I0761166

BRAWLER

Also by Lauren Groff

The Vaster Wilds

Matrix

Florida

Fates and Furies

Arcadia

Delicate Edible Birds

The Monsters of Templeton

For Bill Clegg

BRAWLER

Stories

LAUREN GROFF

Riverhead Books
New York
2026

RIVERHEAD BOOKS
An imprint of Penguin Random House LLC
1745 Broadway, New York, NY 10019
penguinrandomhouse.com

The following stories first published in *The New Yorker*: "The Wind" (2021); "Between the Shadow and the Soul" (2024); "To Sunland" (2022); "Brawler" (2019); "What's the Time, Mr. Wolf?" (2021); "Under the Wave" (2018); and "Annunciation" (2022). "Birdie" first published in *The Atlantic* (2020) and "Such Small Islands" first published in *Small Odysseys* (Algonquin, 2022).

Book design by Amanda Dewey

LIBRARY OF CONGRESS CATALOGING-IN-PUBLICATION DATA
Names: Groff, Lauren author
Title: Brawler : stories / Lauren Groff.
Description: New York : Riverhead Books, 2026.
Identifiers: LCCN 2025021006 (print) | LCCN 2025021007 (ebook) | ISBN 9780593418420 hardcover | ISBN 9780593418444 ebook
Subjects: LCGFT: Short stories
Classification: LCC PS3607.R6344 B73 2026 (print) | LCC PS3607.R6344 (ebook) | DDC 813/.6—dc23/eng/20250624
LC record available at https://lccn.loc.gov/2025021006
LC ebook record available at https://lccn.loc.gov/2025021007

International trade paperback edition ISBN: 9798217183494

Printed in the United States of America
1st Printing

The authorized representative in the EU for product safety and compliance is Penguin Random House Ireland, Morrison Chambers, 32 Nassau Street, Dublin D02 YH68, Ireland, https://eu-contact.penguin.ie.

CONTENTS

BRAWLER

The Wind

Pretend, the mother had said when she crept to her daughter's room in the night, that tomorrow is just an ordinary day.

So the daughter had risen as usual and washed and made toast and warm milk for her brothers, and while they were eating she emptied their schoolbags into the toy chest and filled them with clothes, a toothbrush, one book for comfort. The children moved silently through the black morning, put on their shoes outside on the porch. The dog thumped his tail against the doghouse in the cold yard but was old and did not get up. The children's breath hovered low and white as they walked down to the bus stop, a strange presence trailing them in the road.

WHEN THEY STOPPED by the mailbox, the younger brother said in a very small voice, Is she dead?

The older boy hissed, Shut up, you'll wake him, and all three looked at the house hunched up on the hill in the chilly dark, the green siding half installed last summer, the broken front window covered with cardboard.

The sister touched the little one's head and said, whispering, No, no, don't worry, she's alive. I heard her go out to feed the sheep, and then she left for work. The boy leaned like a cat into her hand.

He was six, his brother was nine, and the girl was twelve. These were my uncles and my mother as children.

MUCH LATER, she would tell me the story of this day at those times when it seemed as if her limbs were too heavy to move and she stood staring into the refrigerator for long spells, unable to decide what to make for dinner. Or when the sun would cycle into one window and out the other and she would sit on her bed unable to do anything other than breathe. Then I would sit quietly beside her, and she would tell the story the same way every time, as if ripping out something that had worked its roots deep inside her.

It was bitterly cold that day and the wind was supposed to rise, but for now all was airless, waiting. After some time, the older brother said, Kids are going to make fun of you, your face all mashed up like that.

My mother touched her eye and winced at the pain there, then shrugged.

They were so far out in the country, the bus came for them first, and the ride to town was long. At last it showed itself, yellow as sunrise, at the end of the road. Its slowness as it pulled up was agonizing. My mother's heart began to beat fast. She let her brothers get on before her and told them to sit in the front seats. Mrs. Palmer, the driver, was a stout lady who played the organ at church, and whose voice when she shouted at the naughty boys in the back was high like soprano singing. She looked at my mother as she shut the bus door, then said in her singsong voice, You got yourself a shiner there, Michelle.

The bus hissed up from its crouch and lumbered off.

I know, my mother said. Listen, we need your help.

And when Mrs. Palmer considered her, then nodded, my mother asked quickly if she could please drop the three of them off when she picked up the Yoder kids. Their mother would be waiting there for them. Please, she said quietly.

The boys' faces were startled, they hadn't known, then an awful acceptance moved across them.

There was a silence before Mrs. Palmer said, Oh, honey, of course, and she shuffled her eyes back to the road. And I won't mark on the sheet that you were missing, neither. So they won't get it together to call your house until second period or so, give you a little time. She looked into the mirror at the boys and said cheerfully, I got a blueberry muffin. Anyone want a blueberry muffin?

We're OK, thanks, my mother said, and sat beside her younger brother, who rested his head on her arm. The fields spun by, lightening to gray, the faintest of gold at the tops of the trees. Just before the bus slowed to meet the cluster of small Yoders, yawning, shifting from foot to foot, my mother saw the old Dodge tucked into a shallow ditch, headlights off.

Thank you, she said to Mrs. Palmer as they got off, and Mrs. Palmer said, No thanks needed, only decent thing to do. I'll pray for you, honey. I'll pray for all of you. We're all sinners who yearn for salvation. For the first time since she rose that morning, my mother was glad, because a person as full of music as the bus driver surely had the ear of god.

The three children ran through the exhaust from the bus as it rose and roared off.

They slid into the warm car, where their mother clutched the steering wheel. She was very pale, but her hair was in its familiar small bouffant. My mother thought of the pain it must have cost my grandmother to do up her hair in the mirror so early in the morning, and felt ill.

YOU DID GOOD, babies, my grandmother said as well as she could, her mouth as smashed as it was. She turned the car. A calf galloped beside them for a few steps in the paddock by the road, and my younger uncle laughed and pressed his hand to the glass.

This is not the time for laughing, my uncle Joseph said sternly. He would grow up to be a grave man, living in an obsessively clean, bare efficiency, teaching mathematics at a community college.

Leave him be, Joey, my mother said. She said in a lower voice to her mother, Poor Ralphie thought you were dead.

Not dead yet, my grandmother said. By the skin of my teeth. She tried to smile at the boys in the mirror.

Where we going? Ralphie said. I didn't know we were going anywhere.

To see my friend in the city, my grandmother said. We'll call when we find a phone out of town. She put a cigarette in her mouth but fumbled with the lighter in her shaky hands until my mother took it and struck the flame for her.

They were going the long way so they wouldn't have to drive past the house again, and my mother watched the minute hand of the clock on the dash, feeling each second pulling her tighter inside.

Faster, Mama, she said quietly, and her mother said without looking at her, Last thing we need's being stopped by one of his buddies. I got to pick up my pay first.

The hospital loomed on the hill beside the river, elegant in its stone facade, and my grandmother parked around back, by the dumpster. Can't risk leaving you, she said. Come with, and bring your stuff. But when she began to walk she could only mince a little at a time, and my mother moved close so she could lean on her, and together they went faster.

They went up the steps through the back door into the kitchen. A man in a ridiculous hairnet like a green mushroom was carrying a pan of peeled potatoes in a bath of water. Without looking he barked, You're late, Ruby. But then the children caught his eye, and he saw the state of them, and he put the potatoes down and reached out and touched my mother's face gently with his hot rough hand. Lord. She get it, too? he said. She's just a kid.

My mother told herself not to cry; she always cried when strangers were tender with her.

Put herself between us. She's a good girl, my grandmother said.

I'll kill the bastard myself, the man said. I'll strangle him if you want me to. Just say the word.

No need, my grandmother said. We're going. But I got to have my check, Dougie. All we got is four dollars and half a tank of gas, and I don't know what I'm going to do if that's all we got to live on.

Can't. No way, Dougie said. Check gets sent to the house, you know this. You filled the form. You checked the box.

My grandmother looked him directly in the face, perhaps for the first time, because she was a timid woman whose voice was low, who made herself a shadow in the world. He sighed and said, See what I can manage, then he disappeared into the office.

Now through the door of the cafeteria there came two women moving fast. One was a plump pretty teenager chewing gum, the cashier, and the other was Doris, my grandmother's friend, freckled and squat and blunt. For extra money, she made exquisite cakes, with flowers like irises and delphiniums in frosting. It was hard to believe a woman as tough as she was could hold such delicacy inside her.

Oh, Ruby, Doris said. It got even worse, huh. Jesus, take a look at you.

Shoved his gun in my mouth this time, my grandmother said. She didn't bother to whisper, because the kids had been there, they had seen it. Thought I was going to be shot. But, no, he just knocked out a few teeth. My grandmother gingerly lifted her lip with a finger to show her swollen bloodied gums. When Doris stepped forward to hug her, my grandmother winced away from her touch, and Doris took the hem of her shirt and lifted it, and said, Oh, shit, when she saw the bruises marbling my grandmother's stomach and ribs.

Better go up and get looked at by a doctor, the cashier said, her damp pink mouth hanging open. That looks real ugly.

No time, my grandmother said. It's already too dangerous to show up here.

In silence, Doris took her cracked leather purse from the hook and put all the cash in her wallet in my mother's hand. The cashier blew a bubble, considering, then sighed and pulled down her own purse and did the same.

Bless you, ladies, my grandmother said. Then she took a shuddering breath and said, In a way, it was my fault. I thought I'd stay until we finished the shearing. You know he's rough with the sheep. I wanted to save them some blood.

Mama? my younger uncle said by the door.

No, don't you do that nonsense, you know that's not right, Doris said, fiercely. It's his fault. Nobody else but his.

Mama? Ralphie said again, louder. It's him, he's here. He pointed out the window, where they could see the nose of the cruiser coming to a stop behind my grandmother's Dodge.

GET DOWN, DORIS SAID, and they all crouched on the tile. They heard a car door slam. Doris, moving faster than seemed possible, went to the door and locked it. Half a second later the knob was rattled, and then there was a pounding, and then my mother couldn't hear for the blood rushing in her ears.

Doris picked up the pan of potatoes and came to the window wearing a furious face. What in hell you want? she shouted. Dare to show your face here.

There was a murmuring, then Doris shouted down

through the glass, Not here, up in the ER getting looked at. Quite a number you done on her. Couldn't hardly walk. She said this nastily, glowering. Then she turned her back on the window and went to the stainless steel table in the middle of the room, where the cashier watched out the window over Doris's shoulder.

They heard an engine starting up, and at last the cashier said in a thick voice, OK, he got in and now he's driving around. But, like, when he figures out you're not up in the ER he's gonna just come into the kitchen through the cafeteria, you know. Like, there's no lock on that door and we can't stop him.

Doris called for Dougie in a sharp voice, and Dougie hurried out of the office with an envelope, looking flushed, a little shamefaced. He had been hiding in there, my mother understood.

I won't forget your kindness, all of you, my grandmother said, but my mother had to take the paycheck because my grandmother's hands were shaking too much.

Send us a postcard when you make it, Doris said. Get a move on.

My grandmother leaned on my mother again and they went out to the car as fast as they could, and it started, and slid the back way, down by the green bridge over the river. When they had twisted out of sight of the hospital, my grandmother stopped the car, opened her door, and vomited on the road.

She shut the door. All right, she said, wiping her mouth gingerly with a finger, and started the car up again.

My mother saw on the dashboard clock that it was just past eight. The teachers were doing roll call right now. Soon a girl would collect the sheets and take them to the office, where someone, thinking they were doing the right thing, would notice that all three of the kids were gone, and call their absence in, first to the house, where the phone would ring and ring. But then, getting hold of nobody, they would call it in to the station, and it would be radioed out immediately to him. And he would know that not only was his wife gone but his kids were gone with her. They had an hour, maybe a bit more, my mother calculated. An hour could maybe take them out of his jurisdiction. She told her mother this, pressing her foot on an imaginary accelerator. My grandmother did drive faster now through the back roads. Gusts of sharp wind pressed the car.

For some time, they were strung into their separate thoughts. My mother counted the cash. A hundred and twenty-three, she said with surprise.

Doris's grocery money, I bet, my grandmother said. Bless her.

Ralphie said sadly, I wish we could've brought Butch.

Yeah, just what we need, your stinky old dog, Joey said.

Can we go back someday to get him? Ralphie said, but my grandmother was silent.

My mother turned around to look at her brothers and said, bitterly, We're never going back. I hope it all burns down with him inside.

Hey, the little boy said weakly. That's not nice. He's my dad.

Mine, too, but I'd be happy if he eats rat poison, Uncle Joseph said. Then he bent forward and looked at the floor, then at the seat beside him, and said, Oh, jeez. Oh, no. Where's your knapsack, Ralphie?

Uncle Ralphie looked all around and said at last, with his eyes wide, I took it into the kitchen but I think I left it.

There was a long moment before this blow hit them all, at once.

Oh, this is bad, my mother said.

I'm so sorry, Ralphie said, starting to cry. Mama, I gotta go pee.

Surely Doris will hide it, my grandmother said.

Hold your bladder, Ralphie. But what if she doesn't find it in time? my mother said. What if she doesn't see it before he does? And he knows that you took us. And he gets on the radio for them all to keep an eye out for us. They could be looking for us now.

My grandmother cursed softly and looked at the rearview mirror. They were whipping terribly fast on the country curves now. The boys, in the back, were clutching the door handles.

My uncle Joey, in a display of self-control that made him seem like a tiny ancient man, said, It's OK, Ralphie, you didn't mean to leave your bag.

My younger uncle reached out his small hand, and Joseph, who hated all show of affection, held it. Ralphie had a fishing accident when I was a teenager, and my cold, dry uncle Joseph fell apart at the funeral, sobbing and letting snot run down his face, all twisted grotesquely in pain.

Mama, we got to get out of the state, my mother said. We'll be safer across state lines.

Shush now, I need to think, my grandmother said. Her hands had gone white on the wheel.

No, what we got to do is ditch the car, my uncle Joseph said. They'll be looking for it. Probably already are. We got to find a parking lot that's full of cars already, like a grocery store or something.

Then what do we do? my grandmother said in a

strangled voice. We walk to Vermont? She laughed, a sharp sound.

No, then we take a bus, Joseph said in his hard, rational voice. We get on a bus and they can't find us then.

OK, my mother said. OK, yeah, Joey's right, that's a good plan. Good thinking. We're fifteen minutes out from Albany, they got a bus station, I know where it is.

It was her father who had once driven her there in his cruiser, because her middle-school choir was taking a bus down to New York City for a competition. He had stopped on the way for strawberry milkshakes. This was a good memory she had of him.

Fine, my grandmother said. Yes. I can't think of nothing else. I guess this will be our change of plans. But, for the first time since the night before, tears welled up in her eyes and began dripping down her bruised cheeks, and she had to slow the car to see through them.

And then she started breathing crazily, and leaned forward until her forehead rested on the wheel, and the car stopped suddenly in the middle of the road. The wind howled around it.

Mama, we need to drive, my mother said. We need to drive now. We need to go.

I really, really have to pee, Ralphie said.

It's OK, it's OK, it's OK, my grandmother whispered. It's just that my body is not really listening to me. I can't move anything right now. I can't move my feet. Oh, god.

It's fine, my mother said softly. Don't worry. You're fine. You can take the time you need to calm down.

And at this moment my mother saw with terrible clarity that everything depended upon her. The knowledge was heavy on the nape of her neck, like a hand pressing down hard. And what came to her was the trail of breadcrumbs from the fairy tale her mother used to tell her in the dark when she was tiny, and it was just the two of them in the bedroom, no brothers in this life, not yet, and the soft, kind moon was shining in the window and her father was downstairs, worlds away. So my mother said, in a soothing voice, So what we're going to do is, Mama's going to take a deep breath and we're going to drive down into Albany, over the tracks, take a right at the feed place, go down by the big brick church, and park in that lot behind it. It's only a block or two from the station. We're going to get out and walk as fast as we can and I'll go in and buy the tickets on the first bus out to wherever, and if we have time I can get us some food to eat on the bus. And we'll get on the bus, and it will slide us out of here so fast. It'll go wherever it's going, but eventually we'll get to the city. And the city is so enormous we can just hide there. And there are museums and parks and movie theaters and subways and everything in the city. And Mama will get a job and we'll go to school and we'll get an apartment and there'll be no more stupid sheep to take care of and it'll be safe. No more having to run out to the barn to sleep. Nobody can hurt us in the city, OK, boys? We're going to have a life that will be so boring, every day it will be the same, and it is going to be wonderful. OK?

By now my mother had pried my grandmother's hands off the steering wheel and was chafing the blood back into them. OK? All we need is for you to take a deep breath.

You can do it, Mama, Joseph said. Ralphie covered his face with both hands. The grasses outside danced under the heavy wind, brushed flat, ruffled against the fur of the fields.

Then my mother prayed with her eyes open, her hands spread on the dash, willing the car forward, and my grandmother slowly put the car back into gear and, panting, began to drive.

This was the way my mother later told the story, down to the smallest detail, as though dreaming it into life: the forsythia budding gold on the tips of the bushes, the last snow rotten in the ditches, the faces of the houses still depressed by winter, the gray clouds that hung down heavily as her mother drove into the valley of the town, the wind picking up so that the flag's rivets on the pole snapped crisply outside the bus station, where they waited on a metal bench that seared their bottoms and they shuddered from more than the cold. The bus roaring to life, wreathed in smoke, carrying them away. She told it almost as though she believed this happier version, but behind her words I see the true story, the sudden wail and my grandmother's blanched cheeks shining in red and blue and the acrid smell of piss. How just before the door opened and she was grabbed by the hair and dragged backward, my grandmother turned to her children and tried to smile, to give them this last glimpse of her.

The three children survived. Eventually they would save themselves, struggling into lives and loves far from this place and this moment, each finding a kind of safe harbor, jobs and people and houses empty of violence. But always inside my mother there would blow a silent wind, a wind that died and gusted again, raging throughout her life, touching every moment she lived after this one. She tried her best, but she couldn't help filling me with this same wind. It seeped into me through her blood, through every bite of food she made for me, through every night she waited, shaking with fear, for me to come home by curfew, through every scolding, everything she forbade me to say or think or do or be, through all the ways she taught me how to move as a woman in the world. She was far from being the first to find it blowing through her, and of course I will not be the last. I look around and can see it in so many other women, passed down from a time beyond history, this wind that is dark and ceaseless and raging within.

Between the Shadow and the Soul

They had lived together for twenty-five years in the old stone house on a bend in the river. They were young when they first saw the place, wildly in love, and so poor they could afford only one of two dwellings in the valley: a battered trailer huddled against the cold wind, and the antique house in foreclosure, a breath from letting the weeds muscle it back into the earth. Willie had wanted the trailer; when you flicked on the lights there, no shower of sparks fell from knob-and-tube wiring. But Eliza had vision. We'll be happy in this house, she said, watching the green river slide through the willows. So they spent the first spring, summer, and fall living in a tent in the largest bedroom, cooking with a propane camper stove and bathing in the river, and they taught themselves how to shingle the roof, to wire and plumb, to plaster and paint and scrape and refinish. Nearly every penny they made went straight into the house; nearly every spare hour was spent on house projects or finding antiques at yard sales and in thrift stores and bringing them back to life.

Time passed. Willie became a high school history teacher, his students' perennial favorite. And one day Eliza realized that she'd been at the village post office for twenty-five years, she was fifty years old and eligible for early retirement. Willie had had too much wine the night she announced she wanted to retire, and he said, recklessly, hopefully, Maybe now we have a kid? This sent an electric zap through her because the question of a kid had not been posed since they had agreed decades ago that they didn't want one. Besides, she was fifty, and did Willie, at forty-three, not understand how women's bodies worked? He saw her face and hastened to say, Oh, obviously adopt, but she was speechless, and his question lingered and began to curdle between them until Willie laughed it off, and said that of course they, just by themselves, were more than enough.

Now he was in the great gnarled apple tree, stringing up fairy lights, which were already plugged in and shining on his face and arms. It was the very end of summer, and across the river the maples were touched at the edges with gold.

Eliza pulled four cherry pies from the oven and set them to cool. She could hear friends coming up the gravel drive and went into the parlor and watched them through the wavy glass, their hands full of flowers, wine, presents. She had not wanted a party, but Willie had insisted. You only retire once, he said, and the house is finally finished—let's show it off. Plus, the new school year would begin on Tuesday, and he wanted a little something festive to mark the end of the summer.

Willie sprang down lightly out of the tree. Thanks to his running and cycling, he was still as lithe as the teenager she'd first loved, even as she had undergone a bit of a midlife spread. Eliza toed the dog away from the screen door and came out with the cheese board in time to overhear her husband saying ruefully, running his hand over his freshly shaved head, Yeah, Eliza told me, oh so delicately, Your golden hair made a promise your scalp could not keep.

The friends laughed—that line always got a big laugh, though it was he, not Eliza, who had said it—then they saw her and cheered. She smiled, kissed them, accepted their praise for the house. It's like cottagecore porn, her new yoga-instructor friend, Mai, said. Jesus Christ, it's straight out of a fairy tale. They placed their tributes in her arms. She accepted the homemade rhubarb butter, the hand-quilted pot holders, the voucher for a master gardening class, although all she really wanted was to crawl into the clean white expanse of her bed.

Music started and beat on into the twilight; the shadows stretched from the roots of the trees. She brought out the giant poached salmon and mayonnaise, the tender green salad from their garden, the barley salad, the focaccia she'd made that morning. People arrived and kept arriving. A rowdy game of badminton began, and the shuttlecocks got lost among the bats fleeting through the dark sky above. The pies were ravaged. Dancing began, oh, god, none of their friends had rhythm, it was astonishing, only Willie danced well, her sprite, her beam of sunshine. He moved her around, and if she danced well also it was simply because she danced with him. When she had to catch her breath, he grabbed any woman close at hand; they were all happy to be spun by him. Under the tables, the dog laid his broad blond head on people's knees and gazed adoringly upward, the slut. Friends kept shouting in Eliza's ear, asking what she was going to do with her days now, and she kept shouting back, Nothing, glorious nothing!

Yes, she coveted it—letting the tea go cold on the kitchen table, the stacks of books, the lazy expanse of days. She had worked every single day since she was small: The flower farm her parents owned had run on the muscle of their three children; away at college, in California, she'd worked in a cafeteria dish room; when she dropped out only a month before graduation it was to take care of her mother, who'd had a debilitating stroke; after her mother died, she worked at the post office; she'd worked on the house weekends and evenings, and she had never in her life had a day of rest.

And as she watched her husband, flushed, so beautiful, so shiny-bald, she understood with a flare of clarity that she had worked so hard in her adult life in part because that was the way she burned off her shame. When she fell in love with Willie, he was sixteen and she was twenty-three, despondent to be back in rural New York changing her mother's diapers, working part-time as a receptionist at the real estate agent's on the corner of Main and Chestnut. She had been so pretty then that they had placed her desk in the window, as if to lure people in. Willie hadn't even gotten his driver's license yet; he was riding his bike to school when he saw her. He dropped the bike and stood staring at her until she shook her head severely at him, mouthing, Go away. Of course she knew who he was. The village was tiny, and there was only one family with a giant Victorian up on the hill and four blond boys in stiff polo shirts; she had gone to high school with his eldest brother, who was now a stockbroker down in the city, like their father. For the next two months, she found tiny nosegays, chocolates, notes on her desk until she capitulated and drove him an hour away to a diner for a date. Oh, she hated herself for starting things up with him, he was only a child, but, in her defense, who wouldn't fall in love with Willie? So bright, so funny, so kind, so handsome. Two years later, he refused to apply to any of the elite schools he could have been accepted to, and went to the state school half an hour away, so that he could move into her mother's house to help her. It caused a great scandal in the village. Some people still had not forgiven her; they would come into the post office, and if she was the only one working, they'd leave without sending their mail.

Someone put on a slow song, and Willie took her hand. His shirt was soaked, and his skin was hot. He kissed her neck. Happy retirement, love, he said. She closed her eyes, pressed her body against his, and her clothes were soon wet with his sweat. Then the music shifted back to Motown, and he shimmied away from her.

Later, when the moon had risen and some of the friends were so drunk that they were resting their heads on the table or lying heaped together in the hammock, she couldn't find Willie. She wandered to the vegetable garden, then down the path brushed by thick dark ferns, to the riverbank. The river always seemed to be speaking in many different voices in a pitch just under her hearing. She stood listening, near the small boathouse she and Willie had built together, until she heard, over the sound of the river, the rhythm, the small grunts, the gasping breaths.

Of course, she thought with a strange calm. She'd known he was too good for her for almost thirty years. And now she was lumpy, spent. It made sense that he would look elsewhere. She stood under the tent of willow branches and listened to the fucking, and her body warmed to it, she became overwhelmed with heat, until the rhythm accelerated and all at once the noises stopped. The sound of hushed laughter. The boathouse door opened. In the shadow of the tree, Eliza pressed her cheek to the bark. She saw svelte, flexible Mai hurry up the path, flinging her cashmere shawl around her shoulders. After a minute or so, in the door, there loomed a dark shape, a man, but, wait, wait, no, he was too tall, too broad, and as he came by her, passing only a foot away, she saw in the moonlight that it was their friend Ben, who owned the hardware store in the village. Happily married, father of three small children. A complicated situation. But not Willie.

SHE LET A FEW MINUTES DISSOLVE in the dark, then went slowly up the path and into the house. She immediately heard her husband in the dining room, telling a story about the stone house's ghost, which had not been happy when the dog had come to them as a puppy. Willie saw her across the room, and she raised her eyes toward their bedroom and went upstairs. He had hired some of their friends' older children to drive any drunk guests home, and car headlights pulsed on the walls in the beautiful pale solitude of their room. She stripped her clothes off and went into the shower. A minute later, Willie slid in with her. Did you like your party? he said. Oh, yes, she said, and reached for him, but he'd had too much to drink and he was not able. Still, he sank to his knees on the tile; she shielded his face from the downpour of hot water with her hand. She bit a washcloth to keep from crying out. They went to bed and held each other even as the music played outside, and the voices shouted and then the music stopped, and their friends either went home or crashed on the couches and floors throughout the house.

Willie fell asleep instantly, but Eliza stayed awake into the silent hours, watching the shimmer of moonbright river on the wall and the ceiling.

Something had started tonight. A pool of darkness had begun to well in her. Long ago, she had lain next to Willie as he slept angelically and she, wracked with misery, had sobbed as quietly as she could. Then, too, she knew she was being absurd. They were in Paris. For two years, they'd saved up money for a honeymoon week there; they'd taken out every book about the city in the village library to prepare; they'd listened to French-language CDs; Willie had taught himself all of Satie's *Gymnopédies* and *Gnossiennes*; Eliza had cooked her way through three Cordon Bleu cookbooks. Their trip was one of radical economy. They stayed in a medieval tower not far from Shakespeare & Co., in a dirty room barely large enough for its single mattress. They had viennoiseries and coffee for breakfast and supermarket picnics for lunch and allowed themselves one hedonistic meal at night, after which they stumbled back drunk over the cobblestones. Sleep like paupers, eat like kings! Willie had said. Paris filled him with manic zest. She would wait in agony all day until he was asleep, and only then would she let herself cry. For her, the glory of the honeymoon had been in the planning, the dreaming, the building up in her mind; what a letdown to find that Paris was just a place, that some days were full of chill gray drizzle, that the dull, thick bodies of other tourists blocked her from full joy. Paris had been a gorgeous dream she had embroidered in her mind—shining, empty, existing for them alone.

Tonight, she was desolate in her bed once more, fifty years old, freshly retired; there would be no children, and the house was at last finished. What she wouldn't give to be in a tight crawl space, sprinkled with squirrel turds, running wire. The profound pleasure of figuring things out, then doing them. All she had to look forward to from now on was rest. One could not build elaborate castles in one's mind out of rest; it was like drawing negative space. Ungrateful, she knew herself to be. But still, she felt the darkness in her grow.

The trees turned to bronze and copper, then stripped themselves skeletal; the cold somehow entered Eliza.

ENOUGH! WILLIE cried out in January, on the third night in a row that he had come home from musical rehearsals at school to find Eliza sitting in the dark at the kitchen table, in the same place where he'd left her, with the same knitting barely touched on her lap. She blinked under the assault of the electric light. My god, Willie said, did you even move? What did you do all day? She shrugged. I watched the meadow, she said. So many tiny changes.

The meadow was a miracle, in fact, the dew frost on the dead brown stalks in the morning, the deer tiptoeing delicately through, the snow flurry that stayed for an hour before the sun burned it off, the birds that seemed to fall down into the grass and burst out of it in sudden sprays, the gorgeous slant of shadows in late afternoon. No purpose in explaining; Willie wouldn't understand. He let the dog out into the twilight to relieve himself. Even when she'd worked all day at the post office, she'd always had a beautiful hot dinner waiting for Willie's return, and now, with oceans of time, she did not. Well, he was capable, he could fend for himself, she thought.

He took off his sport coat, rolled up his sleeves, set to making linguine aglio e olio, and at last put huge plates before each of them, finishing them with Parmesan and pepper. But she could not fathom being hungry. The times she could bear to look at herself in the bathroom mirror, she felt she had gone greige, and now she was the bad kind of thin. She got dizzy going up the stairs to the bedroom.

BABY, HE SAID, blinking fast, I think we have one of two options. Either I take you somewhere to get help, or we find a way to make you start living again.

I am living, she said, winding a fork into her pasta, but it defeated her. She set it down.

Also, he said sternly, you have to bathe every day. You're smelly.

Oh, sorry, she said, and looked down at herself; it was true, she couldn't remember the last time she'd worn anything but Willie's old pajamas.

He launched himself at the problem with his huge energy, and it was clear he'd stayed up for much of the night when he woke her early the next morning with a cup of coffee and a plan. He had gone through the stack of gift cards the friends had given her at the party, months ago, and signed her up for the pottery class, the fiber-arts class, the master gardening class—which had already started, he said, but he had sent a pleading email last night and the instructor had let her in. Also, he'd bought them both gym memberships at the fancy new place half an hour away—they couldn't afford it, especially now that she wasn't working, but oh, well, and he'd be going with her every single day before school and on the weekends, too. We have Pilates at six today, he said. We've got fifteen minutes before we leave, so drink your coffee. I made overnight oats for the car.

It was easier to submit than to resist. In an hour, she found herself with her face pressed against a blue rubber mat, her whole body shaking with the strain, as the Pilates instructor said, Very good, Willie!, and her husband, on his own mat, winked at Eliza.

THE POTTERY CLASS FELT like an old friend, met again after years apart. She had always been good with her hands. The fiber-arts class was artier than anything she'd ever engaged in—she had taught herself how to knit, to crochet, to quilt, even to spin thread from wool—but the instructor showed them images of medieval unicorn tapestries and Gee's Bend quilts and Sheila Hicks's waterfalls and piles of textiles. She encouraged them to think of fiber as a uniquely feminine form of art. Art! What did Eliza, a village postmaster, have to do with art? And she was deeply uncomfortable the first day of the gardening class, held at the university extension, because from the chatter everyone already seemed to know one another. She sat, hunched in her overlarge sweater, angry with Willie. Why in the world did he think this was a good idea? She'd grown up working every single day on a flower farm, for god's sake. What more could she possibly have to learn about plants?

Then the door opened, and in came some kind of young person, tall and heron-thin, in a jumpsuit dirty at the knees, wearing a buzz cut that shone golden under the fluorescents and a gender that was not immediately legible. They crouched beside Eliza and offered a rough hand for her to shake. Bet Dahl, they said, and there was an accent there, intriguing. A scent of dirt and body odor, but not in a bad way. Here's last week's handouts, the instructor said, read them at your leisure at home, and gave Eliza a toothy smile that turned the austere face suddenly soft and dimpled.

Eliza was knocked out of her composure. Bet stood at the front of the class and said, Compost! Today we learn how to make it. On Thursday, in the greenhouses, we will put into practice what we have learned. Tell me what you already know. The group clamored to answer, and Eliza counted her breaths until she could hear what was being said.

Bet, it turned out, was short for Betina. She was a PhD student writing a dissertation on native gardening in the North American Northeast. Originally from Utrecht. On the drive home through the dark that night, Eliza saw in her mind's eye thick rows of tulips in color blocks stretching to the horizon, like a modern painting, a bony figure on a bicycle cutting through them, a windmill in the distance. She wondered if Bet had turned to native plants in reaction against the artificial beauty of Dutch tulips. A revolt against order. She imagined Bet in her apartment in the small university town thirty miles from her stone house: The place would have clean white walls, lots of light, plants in every window, a mattress on the floor. Bet would not care about aesthetics. She would not see the old linoleum in the kitchen. She would own only what was needed. No decades accumulated in the drawers. A life kept fresh.

At home when Eliza came in, Willie looked at her hopefully over the stir-fry spitting in the wok, and she said, keeping her voice neutral, Yes, I think I'll like the gardening class.

On Tuesdays they had in-class learning in the extension rooms; on Thursdays they had their practicums at the university greenhouses and fields. Eliza had always been strong—she'd had to be to fix up their house, to sling packages all day at the post office—but she'd let her muscles turn to goop since she had retired. She was a weak little slug now. She nearly cried in the greenhouse when she went to slide a forty-gallon citrus tree and a classmate, Don, a strangely handsome orthodontist, had to step in to help her. At the gym, in the morning, even though her whole body protested, she started staying for the session that followed Pilates, no matter what it was, HIIT or barbells or spin, pushing through her dizziness and nausea, averting her eyes from the mirrors when she changed in the locker room.

In each of her classes, by the second week, the mass of participants had separated into individuals. In pottery, there was a couple who owned the café in town; in fiber arts, she hit it off with a grave, soft-cheeked new mother. In the gardening class, there was orthodontist Don, retired librarians Norma and David, goofy young Eagle Scout Mikey, and a grandmother, mother, and daughter named Linda, Janet, and Julia. In the frozen months, they were each to plan a native garden; in March, they would plant; in June, there would be a field trip to visit all of their projects. Eliza wanted to use a space at the top of the stone house's meadow, south-facing, for her garden. She decided that her patch would be all edible native plants, as carefully designed as an ornamental garden; she would grow groundnuts on trellises, hibiscus like roses, jewelweed with the little green pods that explode, dooryard violet as ground cover. What joy it was to be dreaming in pictures, to be deep in research.

In the greenhouse one Thursday in late February, as she was transferring the cuttings and poking in the seeds, the soil in the pots looked so rich that she couldn't control herself, she thrust her fingers deep into it. Warm and soft. She laughed to herself. A voice in her ear, Bet, behind her, said, Irresistible, yes, sometimes I am compelled to do that also. Eliza went so hot in the face that she had to step outside into the blustery evening to cool off. When she came back in, she avoided Bet's eye. That time of life, eh, murmured Linda, the grandmother of the trio of women. Nobody ever tells you it's hell.

No! Eliza wanted to protest; she was too young. But that was not the truth, was it? Yet another thing about her body to be ashamed of, she thought, and she felt tenderly for her poor aging self.

That weekend, at the grocery store, Eliza hovered near the cosmetics wall and, almost without looking, tossed in mascara, concealer, lip gloss, and sped to the checkout, feeling furtive. In the parking lot, she ran into Mai, who threw her arms into the air and shouted, Jesus Christ! You've lost, like, forty pounds!, and kissed the air beside Eliza's ears, then hurried off somewhere, probably to seduce a married man. In the car on the way home, the day surprisingly mild, Eliza opened the windows and sang along to the radio, scaring the neighbor's sheep into a trot as she wailed by.

In March, after the practicum in the greenhouse, Don suggested they all go for a drink after class, and everyone but young Mikey squeezed into a booth in a tavern up the road. Eliza's leg was up against Bet's wiry thigh. Every time Bet reached for her beer, Eliza felt it in her shoulder. She laughed too wildly at Norma and David's shtick, and she drank too quickly. When she overcame her shyness enough to tell a joke, Bet squeezed her knee under the table while everyone laughed, and her body responded in a rush, and afterward, for minutes at a time, she could not hear the conversation as it moved on without her. Her hand shook when she lifted her wine to her mouth. At midnight, the dark road swerved in the windshield on the way home. When she climbed out of the car, she didn't want to go into the house, past the dog groaning on his bed in the kitchen, through the dark parlor, up the stairs, into the bedroom where Willie was sleeping. Instead, she stood for a long while out in the clear, cold air, smelling all the new green in the world, feeling the sap rising, the trees awakening, the tender grass just now showing itself in the fields. Her old friend the river spoke loudly, swollen with snowmelt and spring rain.

SHE STOOD THERE for such a long time, exultant, that she began to shiver, and the dog whined at the door for her to just come in already. And she was up before Willie in the morning, so overflowing with energy that she made them fried-egg sandwiches for the ride to the gym, and the dog followed her, his forehead furrowed, as she paced from room to room, until it was time to wake her husband.

Then it was April, and when Bet gave the class her cell number so that they could call her when they were preparing and planting their native plots, Eliza put it into her phone as Florist, without explaining to herself what she was doing. As if Willie would care! Besides, she had done nothing wrong. And he had his own preoccupations, so busy with the school musical, his voice raspy from calling out corrections to the actors on the stage. The refrigerator full of takeout boxes because neither of them came home before nine most nights. The dog bore a look of patient despondency.

One Sunday in late April, she was out in the morning mist, kneeling in the earth in her plot, when Willie knelt beside her and took up a spade and began to dig. She was startled out of her reverie—a strange erotic daydream, flesh without body, warmth without a face. Willie couldn't see inside her head, she told herself; besides, daydreaming hurt nobody. She watched his strong square hands with the golden hairs on his knuckles as he dug one giant hole for a hibiscus plant, then another. Are you all right? he said at last, chopping through a fibrous root. You've seemed so far away from me.

She rose up on her knees, brushed the hair out of her eyes with the back of her hand. Look at me, she said. I look and feel better than I have in decades.

He peered at her over his shoulder. You do, he said, but sadly.

What? she said, and waited, and her irritation with his slowness grew, and was just about to tip into anger when at last he said, You'll tell me when you're ready.

She felt cold then, and she wondered if he had seen her texts with Bet. But there was nothing there to alarm him other than the sheer volume—it was just a lot of jokes and photos of plants, a thrilled flurry yesterday when, on a hike with the dog in the forest, Eliza had found a cluster of chanterelles.

Wasn't this what he had wanted? Her, bursting with life?

Willie, she said, you told me to live, I'm living—I don't know what to say.

He in his turn said nothing more, just left the spade embedded to the handle in the ground and went back to the house, and the dog abandoned her to run off behind him.

At the tavern after gardening class now, Eliza stayed beyond the slow trickle of people going home, so that most nights it was her and Bet and Julia, the plain, sarcastic twentysomething daughter of the grandmother-mother-daughter trio, who remained until the bartender dipped the lights and began stacking the chairs. One night, Eliza and Julia stood in the parking lot, watching Bet stride off to her apartment up the street, until Julia sighed and flicked her cigarette so the sparks tumbled redly across the asphalt, and when Eliza turned away the girl said in a contemptuous voice, Don't get a DUI on your way home.

Excuse me? Eliza said, and the girl said, You're excused, and vanished into her car before Eliza could tell her to grow up. Julia apologized to Eliza the next Tuesday with a canister of peanut butter cookies that Eliza shared with the class. I was just frustrated, Julia said, but with what Eliza chose not to ask. All class, she watched the girl out of the corner of her eye, but Bet didn't flirt with her more than she flirted with anybody, including young Mikey and the married librarians; certainly less than she flirted with Eliza.

MAY WAS UPON THEM too soon. The leaves were vivid, the sky clear, the cherry trees so frilly they could break your heart.

For her final project in fiber arts, Eliza had decided

to go overlarge, cheeky, knitting a postal-service mailbag out of hot-pink yarn and overstuffing it with junk mail until it nearly burst. Was this art? What was art, anyway? But the instructor seemed pleased and solemn and, in the end-of-class show, hung the work where visitors to the gallery saw it first thing. Of all her pottery creations, Eliza took home only a single large vase and a bowl; everything else seemed imperfect to her. When she left, the rest of the class was dividing up the cups and bowls and vases she didn't want. Take the advanced class in the fall? the teacher said quietly, holding the door open for her, and Eliza said, Maybe. In truth, she thought of very little these days but her plants pushing up out of the ground, the heat and steam of the greenhouse, Bet and her rain of photos of joe-pye weed and Queen Anne's lace, her affectionate touches of Eliza's waist, her arm, her back. One night in the tavern, Bet pressed unnecessarily close as she was going into the bathroom and Eliza was going out. The wicked grin, the earthy smell. Then the door closed and Eliza was alone in the hallway, lightning coursing through her.

The final class would be on the first Saturday morning of June. They would visit each plot of land to see how the gardens were coming along and finish at Don's house for lunch. Potluck? Janet said, and Don said, No, no, it'd be my honor to feed you, don't worry.

They started at the greenhouses because Mikey, Linda, Janet, and Julia didn't have space at home for a garden. Only Linda's was interesting, Eliza thought, with its intentional clashes of color; the rest were a random scattering of droopy, unloved plants. Norma and David had converted the median strip beyond their sidewalk into a native-plant repository—Christmas fern, aster, monarda, bergamot. It was smart. It would be beautiful by August. Eliza was nervous as she led everyone over the country roads to the stone house. Willie was out on a long bike ride, she knew; she had timed it carefully. When they arrived, Norma and David were in ecstasy, young Julia had a pinched expression on her face, and Bet looked at Eliza and smiled. I could live forever in a place like this, she said.

ELIZA LED THEM UP to the meadow. Her native garden hadn't grown as much as she'd hoped, but it was still quite lovely, with arching trellises she'd built and paths mowed through the design. She brought up a pitcher of homemade lavender lemonade, and people drank and exclaimed, and the dog darted around, and they lingered until Don said, at last, I'm almost reluctant to tear us away, but my wife is texting madly that lunch awaits us.

When they came down from the meadow, Willie was back from his ride and showered and standing barefoot on the slate walk. So this is the famous group, he said, and his eyes darted from face to face, coming to rest on Don's. The more the merrier, Don said. Come along with us to lunch.

Oh, Eliza started to say, Willie's got plenty to do, but he said, With pleasure!, and slipped on his shoes and put himself into the car.

Don's place was only ten minutes away. Eliza didn't know what she was expecting but certainly not a vast iron gate, a drive up through poplars, a house so massive it could have been a château. Teeth bought this? Eliza said, and Willie said thoughtfully, His name is Don Fisher? I bet he's a Fisher from the family that used to own hundreds of thousands of acres up here. So not teeth. This is generational wealth. Willie looked grim.

Don's wife was on the drive to meet them. She was tiny and blond, and her face was frozen stiff when she smiled. She wore a whole equestrienne outfit, down to the boots.

Don't know about you, but I'm starving, Don said, and led them through the great mirrored hallway into a very large dining room with a buffet of soups and salads and sandwiches on the sideboard. I didn't know what people liked, Don's wife said, so I had the cook make everything!

They sat, and before they started eating, Don stood and gave a long and impassioned speech about the class, the camaraderie he had found there, about the brilliance of Bet, who had just successfully defended her PhD thesis. Then Don handed around flutes of champagne, and they raised a glass to the teacher. On one side of Eliza, Willie put his hand on hers, and on the other, under the table, Bet's knee pressed against her knee. She had to close her eyes and breathe. They ate, and the cook darted behind them and filled glasses with white or red wine, even for Mikey, who drank his down in two gulps before anyone could stop him.

They were all tipsy when they went into the soft gray day to the garden. Willie walked ahead of Eliza, and Bet hip-checked her, and they laughed. Don's gardens were frankly astonishing: He had his own greenhouse full of orchids, and he had two gardeners standing there, grinning. His native-plant plot was more elaborate than Eliza's but not, she was happy to discover, more beautiful. The garden was so large that the class soon fragmented, the trio of women going over to the rose garden in full blush, the librarian couple going to the potager with its espaliered pears, Mikey heading down to a pond where a swan glided between reeds.

Eliza crouched to look at a blue lobelia, and when she looked up Willie was not beside her. She could see nobody but the librarians in the distance.

SHE STOOD, a dark feeling spreading in her. She thought of Willie, where he would go, and hurried back to the greenhouse. She came in softly. Yes, there was his voice. She stood in the doorway, listening.

I thought it was Don, Willie was saying. All afternoon. But it's not. It's you.

Me what? Bet's voice said, sharply. They were hidden from Eliza by a palm made gaudy with orchids.

Oh, please, Willie said.

Bet said, It is always like this. But nothing happened. It's a big nothing. I flirted, yes, but I flirt with everyone. I flirt with Mikey, I flirt with Linda, who's maybe eighty. But she is so timid, your Eliza, I waited, and she flirted back, but she made no move. And, even if something did happen, what's it to you? You don't own her.

We've been together forever, Willie said. We're married.

There was a long pause, and Bet's voice changed. OK, she said. You are suffering. I am not cruel. So I say now that I am not interested in Eliza. These old wives, they're fun for a month, then they get clingy and crazy. I promise . . .

But Eliza didn't stay to hear what Bet promised. She hurried up the path and back into the house. She ran cold water on her wrists in the bathroom, and then she came back to the dining room, where a giant glossy cake bedecked in real flowers waited on the table. She saw the champagne bottles in their frosty buckets and took a full one with her to the window seat and sat behind the velvet curtain. She gulped, letting the champagne spill onto her chin and neck. She replaced the drained bottle with a full one, and hunched over her knees behind the curtain until the others came back inside, and there was another speech by Don and the clinking of forks on plates, then voices saying goodbye. The windows darkened. She felt slightly better in the shadows. She heard Willie calling for her but did not care to respond. At last, the pale mask of Don's wife peeked around the curtain, and she called out in a voice made high-pitched with fear and relief, She's here.

Hey, Willie said, sitting next to her. He took the mostly empty bottle from her hand. Ready to go home? Everyone left a while ago.

And he helped her to stand, and said a very cheery

thank-you to Don and his wife, who nodded graciously, and Willie put Eliza into the car and buckled her in and pulled back through the great gates.

She found that her face was extremely hot, but it didn't have to be shame; it could have been a hot flash. The landscape undulated by. They went across the bridge toward their house, shining in the twilight, and as they passed a boat launch she said urgently, Pull over, stop.

She got out of the car and tripped running down to the launch and skinned her hands, but she was up again before Willie could come around to help her. At the river, she stripped off all her clothes, not caring who could see her nakedness from the bridge. She jumped in.

The current was muscular, the water delicious, dark blue. Willie came in after her. She floated on her back, and Willie joined her, taking her hand, until the current swept them past the bridge. They slowly breaststroked back in silence, and dressed, shivering, and rode with the windows down until the stone house appeared glowing up the drive.

The dog danced his happiness to see them. Willie bent to greet him. Eliza escaped upstairs, took off her wet clothes, and lay naked, splayed, grotesque on top of the covers. She didn't bother to wipe the hot tears away, and they ran into her ears.

In time, she became aware that Willie had come up to the room and was sitting in the armchair in the corner, watching her. She'd found the antique chair on the side of the road and had upholstered and refinished it herself. Everything in this house she'd touched and made her own. She hated it all. She saw herself as her husband must see her now, sloppy, spilling over the bed, old, no longer as coltishly beautiful as she'd once been; well, her legs had made a promise her genes couldn't keep. She stole a look at his face. She'd seen that expression before. Oh, yes, it had been the first time she'd become aware of Willie as a person. She'd been eleven, he'd been four or thereabouts, and her parents were having their annual Fourth of July party at the flower farm. The beer ball was submerged in ice, the table was full of other families' Tupperware, her father was not dead yet, he was presiding over the grill, making countless hot dogs and hamburgers. She was sitting on the dock of the swimming hole, so thick with thrashing children that she felt indignant; it was her water, her pond. Through the gate walked Willie's family, his father with that swoop of blond hair, his bone-thin mother in her long skirt and cardigan on this hot day, the four small boys in matching yellow polo shirts. Willie was the youngest. The three older boys had gone to the table and were quietly wolfing down as much as they could fit in their mouths; they were wealthy, but their mother had a strange relationship with food, and there was never enough in the house. Willie had gone to the dock. He had slipped off a moccasin and stood next to Eliza, dipping a toe in the water.

His father had gravitated to the grill and was holding a pair of tongs in his hand, and now he called out in a stern voice, William, I said no swimming. Conversation lulled; the music seemed louder. Willie bit his lower lip, and then took off his other shoe.

William, his father said in a very loud voice now, and started across the grass. Just before his father reached him, Willie tipped sideways and into the pond, fully clothed.

His father reached over and yanked him out by the arm and everyone heard the crack, but the boy didn't scream, and his father carried him by the arm for ten feet, tossed aside the tongs he was still holding, put Willie down, pushed him in the middle of the back, and said in a curt voice, We're going. The mother picked Willie up, still dripping, the boy's arm doing a funny thing, his face buried in her neck. The three older sons shoved food into their pockets and ran after their parents.

Things happened in Willie's house, and the whole town knew, but nobody ever did anything about it.

Those things pulsed there at the center of her husband, deep-rooted, the source of his willful goodness, what he'd wanted to avoid when he'd taken her hand early on and gently said that he was sorry, he would never have children, he would understand if this was a deal-breaker.

Just before the four-year-old Willie had let himself fall into the dark water, he had looked at Eliza, and she'd seen on his face what she saw there forty years later—sorrow, and rage, and a kind of mad, obstinate joy.

She was a fool. She could not leave this man. Who would take care of him then. Oh, but she hadn't wanted to leave him, not really, had she. She had just wanted to know what it was like to brush up against the dazzling future again. She felt the part of her that the lush spring had stirred to life go dormant, deep in her, once more. She knew that it would not awaken again in her lifetime. She opened her arms to her husband and waited. He took his time, but at last he came to her, as she knew he would. He put his head under her chin, and his breath was warm on her neck, and, like this, she held him until he slept.

To Sunland

He woke to an angry house and darkness in the windows. Aunt Maisie had packed his suitcase the night before and left it near the front door, and so he dressed himself without turning on the light and came out and dropped the pajamas on top of the suitcase. She was in the kitchen, banging the pans around.

Buddy, she said when she saw him, set yourself down and get some of this food in you. Her eyes were funny, all red and puffy, and he didn't like to see them like that. When he sat down, she came up behind him and hugged his head so hard it hurt, and her hands smelled like soap and cigarettes and grease, and he pulled away.

HE ATE HER EGGS, which were like his mother's eggs, though her biscuit was not like his mother's biscuit; it was too dry, and there was no tomato jam. When he was finished, she took his plate and fork and washed them.

I can't stand it, she said. I will never forgive that girl, not as long as I live.

All right, he said softly.

I can't stay around to watch this, she said. You get your shoes and coat on. I'm going in to work early so's I don't have to look that selfish, wicked girl in the face. She gathered her own things and swiped a thin red line of lipstick on her mouth, then took her car keys from the hook and went out the front door. There she bent to put his pajamas in his suitcase, and said impatiently, You come on outside, Buddy. That rocking chair's comfortable enough for you to wait in, I wager. I'll get you a jelly jar of water. You need to relieve yourself, get down off the porch and do it in the azaleas.

Now he was outside in the darkness, and the smell of the orange blossoms was all around. The light above Aunt Maisie's front door was thick with termites that were flying in and out of the beam.

Aunt Maisie came out again with water for Buddy and locked her front door, and for a second, as she leaned toward the lock, in the dim light her hair was the same as his mother's hair, and he forgot, and thought she was his mother, and he nearly cried out in gladness.

Then she looked up at him and it was with Aunt Maisie's face. The gladness died in him and he began to cry.

Now don't you start blubbering, Aunt Maisie said. You'll set me off again. Big like a man and twenty years old, but you're just a little old baby in your head, poor soul.

No, ma'am. I'm a man, he said, and wiped his face.

Because he was much taller than her, she waited until he sat in the rocking chair, then she leaned in and kissed him on the cheek. You be good, Buddy, she said. Get down on your knees and pray every night like your mama taught you. Don't you be making no trouble, you hear?

Yes, ma'am, he said.

I'll write you every week on Sunday and try to get myself up there to visit once a month or so, depending on my money. You know I don't make barely enough for my own food and, besides, I'm getting old now, not doing so good myself these days. Well, no more of that. In any event, don't forget there's a soul in the world that loves you. That's right, your aunt Maisie loves you, she said.

Yes, ma'am, he said.

She dug in her pocketbook and put a note under the handle of his suitcase. Now you be sure your sister sees that note whenever she turns up, you hear? She smiled, but it wasn't a smile, really.

Yes, ma'am, he said, and began moving in the rocking chair as she went down the steps and into her car, and the headlights were too bright for a minute, until she backed all the way out into the road and was gone.

He did not feel the cold so much when he rocked. He was soothed by the orange blossoms hiding out there in the darkness, the golden rain of termites, the noises of some night bird calling somewhere, the good rhythm of his rocking. It was nice to see the way the sky began to take on a pale line at its edge, then pink began to grow out of the pale line and spun up and out, and he could see the orange groves out there coming clear in the new light. Then the sun rose full, and though he knew enough not to look at it for very long, he did look at it a little bit, and when he closed his eyes the sun shone in echoing red on his lids. Now the fog was lifting up from the ground under the trees and an animal he didn't know the name of, shiny and hard-looking with a long tail, moved slowly through the yard, sniffing at things.

Then, all at once, there was Joanie in the morning light in front of him, her own suitcase in her hand and a straw hat with a yellow band on her head. She had walked up without him seeing or hearing her. She was frowning. Hey there, Bud, she said. Aunt Maisie isn't here with you? She left you out here all by your lonesome? She jutted her chin at the house, and he turned to look but there was no one there. Then she saw the note under the suitcase's handle and pulled it out and read it and gave a sharp laugh. She balled the note up and threw it down on the worn rubber doormat.

She feels so dang strong about it, maybe she could've kept you herself, Joanie said. That old bat-faced shrew. She took a white handkerchief out of her pocketbook and spat on a corner, then rubbed at his face where he still wore Aunt Maisie's kiss. You ready to walk a bit? she said.

Yes, Joanie, he said, and stood and chuckled as the rocking chair rocked on without him in it.

She took his suitcase in one hand and hers in the other and led him down the path to the soft, thick dirt of the road. They went for a long time through the stretch with laurel oak trees and palmettos on one side, the big plantation of orange trees on the other. It was early enough that there was some shade, and they kept to it. Joanie seemed to be thinking about something and didn't talk, which was all right, because he liked to watch her two braids snake back and forth across her back as she walked.

When they got to the turnoff toward the fishing

camp, she put the suitcases down with a sigh and shook out her hands. At this rate, she said, we're not going to make the noon bus. Then she looked at him where he stood and said, Hey, wait, what am I thinking? You're pretty strong, right, Buddy?

Real strong, he said, and he picked up the suitcases as if they were nothing.

They went on through the sun spots and the shade and were almost at the crossroads when a sound came from behind them, and a pickup barreled past in a big blow of dust. Then the truck stopped and blinked its back lights and reversed toward them. Joanie swore under her breath and patted her hair but was smiling when the driver rolled down his window. He was a red-faced man with eyes hidden under the brim of his cap. Well, if it isn't Joanie Greene, the driver said.

In the flesh, she said. And her big old brother, Buddy. How you doing, Mr. Summerlin? You're not going into town, are you? I like your new truck.

Looks like I am now, he said. I was only driving around in my brand-new baby, just now picked her up from the lot. She's a fifty-six, last year's model, so I got her for a song. Anyways, since you've graduated you know you can call me Harmon.

Thanks, Harmon, she said. Saving us a long, hot walk.

Toss them suitcases in the back and climb up right next to me, girl, he said. You and your brother. How's it going, Buddy? I heard a bunch of rumors about you, but your mama kept you to her own self, didn't she.

Yessir, Buddy said, and put the suitcases into the bed of the truck.

Speaking of which, the driver said as they climbed in and Joanie reached across Buddy's lap to close the door, I'm sorry for your loss, both of you.

Thank you, Joanie said. We didn't get along so great all the time, but it's still not easy to lose a mother.

The truck started moving, and the wind felt so good on Buddy's cheeks that he closed his eyes. Joanie told the driver how their mother had barely left them anything. The bank had come in and taken away the house, and Joanie had to scramble to sell off everything before it was put out on the street. Humiliating, she said. All my mama's old-lady friends haggling with me over pieces of her embroidery, her clock, her teapot. Like vultures. Trying to get as much out of me for as little money as possible.

Girl, the driver said, you know that if you need help all you got to do is ask. We can work something out. And he looked at Buddy out of the corner of his eye and slowly put one of his big red hands on Joanie's knee.

Joanie laughed and didn't pull her knee away. You're

a good guy, Harmon, she said. But you see we got our suitcases. We're getting out of this old dump.

Where to? he said.

She said, Guess.

Huh, he said, and looked across at Buddy. Something new came into his face, and he said, You taking him to the Colony up in Gainesville. That place for the feebleminded and epileptic. Well, well. Isn't that something. Everybody always said how your mama should have done it years ago.

I am, yeah, she said. I wrote away and got a letter back that they're holding a place for him. They started calling it something else, though. Sunland. Sounds softer.

And you staying up there? Harmon said. Getting yourself a job, becoming a real career girl?

Nah, Joanie said, and a smile played on her lips and she said, Surely you remember how smart I am.

Top of your class, he said. A whip-cracker. Run rings around the rednecks in this place.

Anyways. Last year I applied to all the ladies' colleges up north and I got my pick. Took the one that gave me a full scholarship, up there in Maine. Then my mama got sick and they let me defer and come for the spring semester. Got me a train ticket and a hundred-dollar bill and just a bit more to get me there and set up with books before school starts in about a week.

Jesus. Maine, he said. Practically the North Pole. You're going to freeze your Florida fanny off, girl.

That's the idea, she said. Give me igloos and whale blubber. I'd go to another planet if I could.

Well, congratulations, Harmon said, and his hand slid a little farther up her thigh and some of his fingers disappeared under her skirt. You know, I heard about you, Joanie Greene. I know some people around here will be missing you sorely.

She pushed his hand back down to her knee and said, Ah, Harmon, come on, now.

They were nearing the barn at the edge of town that had a life-size plaster bull on its roof, and Buddy leaned forward eagerly and put his finger on the windshield and shouted out, Bull!

The other two laughed, and Joanie said, Yep, Buddy, that's a bull. She took Buddy's big hand in her small one and squeezed it.

Hey, listen, the driver said too quickly as they came close to the bus station. You got some time before the bus leaves, maybe we can drop Buddy off to sit for a spell on a bench there and you and me can drive somewheres for a little chat. Give you a goodbye to remember. Make you think of your old hometown in a positive light when you're up there in Maine.

Joanie didn't lose her smile, but it went tight and she said, Nah, thanks for the offer, but we don't have all that much time.

The truck stopped and she leaned over Buddy and opened the door and pushed him out. Grab them suitcases, Bud, she said in a low voice, and then she went around to the driver's window and murmured there for a bit. Buddy watched from the shade as the pleasantness fell off the driver's face and he began to look red and then angry, and then he pulled out his wallet and handed over some bills to Joanie, who tucked them into her pocketbook. The driver threw the pickup into reverse and drove away far too fast, spitting dust up all over them.

Never coming back to this old snake pit again, she said, might as well make a little money setting fire to all my bridges. Still can't believe they let that old lecher work at the high school.

She sighed and smacked dust off her skirt and blouse and hat, and said, Anyways, we got about a half hour, what do you say we go get ourselves a milkshake, and led Buddy into the drugstore where their mother used to take him for lunch after church on Sundays.

There was nobody in the drugstore besides the boy

in the paper cap behind the counter, who flushed when he saw Joanie come in. Hey there, Buddy! he called out in a strange, strained voice. You here for your usual? Burger, chocolate malted?

Oh, yes, please, Buddy said, putting down the suitcases and sitting on a stool. His stomach rumbled loudly.

Hey there, Joanie, the boy said, flicking his eyes at her. Haven't seen you for a spell. You doing good? You looking good.

Well, I'm an orphan now. So not so good, I guess, she said dryly.

Ah, jeez. Oh, boy, the boy said, and his blush became almost purple. I'm so sorry, Joanie. I didn't know. Was wondering why your mama didn't bring Buddy in here this last month or so. Ah, man, I'm such a pumpkin head. Listen, I'll make it up to you. I'll buy you lunch. It's on me. Well, it's on Mr. Katz who owns the place, but he'll never know. And the boy winked and turned away and began fiddling with the grill, shaking his head once in a while and hissing under his breath at his own stupidity.

Joanie smiled to herself then, but every time the boy stole a glance at her she put a sad expression on her face.

Buddy looked at himself in the mirror behind the syrups. He liked his dark hair and dark eyes, but he did not like the dust that was in his hair. It kept being a surprise to him that it was Joanie next to him in the mirror, carefully shaking the dirt out of her clothing and her hair and dabbing at her face with a paper napkin, and not his mother. Every time, the surprise turned to pain.

The boy in the paper hat delivered two malteds, two burgers, and two fries, and hovered as they ate. Buddy was so hungry he barely chewed, and Joanie ate delicately, touching the corners of her mouth with her napkin after every bite. When Buddy was done, he looked at her food so hard that she pushed it over to him.

Wasn't good? the boy said anxiously. You didn't like it, Joanie?

Don't you fret, Joanie said, it was wonderful. I just haven't been eating much recently and it takes only a few bites to fill me up.

Nice to hear you thought it was good, the boy said, but then the bells above the door jingled and an old couple, arm in arm, came in and sat down on the stools. He rolled his eyes and went over with his little pad of paper to take their order.

Buddy finished all the food. Joanie wiped his face and hands. She slid off the stool and dug into her pocketbook for a quarter. Then she reconsidered, replaced the quarter, and put a dime on the counter.

Let's go, she said to Buddy.

But they hadn't gone more than a few steps before the boy rushed back to where they'd sat and said, Hey, Joanie, hey, Joanie, wait a second, do you maybe want to go out with me one of these days? I can borrow my brother's car. We'll go for a drive, maybe get some dinner, maybe. Or go bowling or fishing or something.

Joanie turned around with a broad smile on her face and said, Oh, I'd love that, truly. Why don't you just call my aunt Maisie's house for a date? She don't like me going out with boys, so she'll try to tell you I don't live there, but don't you listen, just keep calling and one day you'll get me, not her.

Oh, great, Joanie, the boy said, I'll do that. I'll just keep calling for you.

You do that, she said, and she and Buddy went outside and Joanie laughed as they crossed the road. Oh, boy, she said. Maisie's going to get so mad.

Yes, Buddy said, and laughed, not because he understood but because his sister was laughing and the sound made him happy.

But soon he saw that something was wrong, and he stopped and put down the suitcase. Home is this way, he said slowly, pointing down the street full of dusty magnolias. Church this way, he said, pointing at the big redbrick church on the corner.

Joanie shaded her eyes and looked at him and said

gently, We're not going to church or home, Bud. We're off on a bus to Gainesville.

Oh, he said. I don't know that place.

Me neither, she said. Well, we lived up there when we was real small, but when Daddy left Mama so sudden she took a strong dislike to the place, brought us down to this dumb little nothing town.

I want Mama, Buddy said, and began to cry.

Ah, none of that, Buddy, she said. None of that right now. Big old boy blubbering in the street. As if it's not hard enough as it is. And she put the suitcase back in his hand, and took his other hand and pulled him through the parking lot to where the bus was already grumbling and people were slowly climbing up into it.

The bus was broiling hot and they had to go halfway back to find a seat, but Joanie said it'd be cool once they were moving and wind came through the windows. She parked their suitcases on their laps, because, she said in a whisper, you can't trust none of the people who ride buses. All the people you can trust already have their own cars and wouldn't be caught dead in a bus. Someday, she said dreamily, she was going to buy herself a great big car, pearly colored, with leather so soft inside you'd think you were riding along in a cool white bed.

But Buddy wasn't listening, because among the people getting on the bus was a woman with a great puff of red hair under a very tiny hat, and in one hand she held a blue suitcase and in the other a golden cage with two crested cockatiels in it. She was heavy, and gasping, and she stopped for a minute at the seat opposite Buddy and Joanie's, then scanned her options and sighed, and put the cage next to the window and settled herself down.

The driver came on and took people's quarters. Joanie cursed under her breath but opened her pocketbook and dug around for change. Bleeding me dry, she said to Buddy. Guess I won't be eating until I get to Maine.

The lady across the way overheard her, and said, Maine? You two running off to Maine? I come up on this bus and I see you here and I think, Look at that handsome boy, that pretty girl, I bet they're sweethearts running off together, how romantic. And I says to myself, Ada Severin, you sit yourself down right next to them there, see if you can't get their story, maybe you know their people, but then the closer up to you I get, the more I see that no, they're not sweethearts, not at all, maybe they're brother and sister, there's a family resemblance around the eyes, and then by the time I get here I see clear that there's something funny going on with that handsome boy right there, maybe something not quite right up in his brain.

Don't you say that. Everything's just perfect in his brain, Joanie said sharply. He's all angels and rainbows up there. His gears are just slower than most.

In any event, the lady said with a chesty sort of laugh, not often that I'm wrong. Blessed Jesus has bestowed upon me the power of perception. I always had it, I guess you'd say, but it got sharpened when I started reading them Sherlock Holmes books in the library. What you do is you look real hard at a person and see all the tiny things and then put them together. Like, the bus driver has those deep scars on his hands, you see them? I bet he was a turpentine cutter up in the pines for a long while. But he has a little hitch in his walk, and I bet an accident happened and that's why he started driving buses.

Maybe so, Joanie said. Maybe not.

Say, the lady said in an excited voice, he's coming back this way. Let's see if I'm right. She said to the bus driver, Pardon me, but we got a little wager going that you used to be a turpentine cutter up in them pines once upon a time.

The driver stopped in the aisle and looked down at the lady's face for a long moment. At last he said, gravely, I don't believe I know you, ma'am, and kept going to his seat at the front.

See? the lady crowed. Told you.

Neither confirmation nor denial, Joanie said. I think he gave you the old mind your own beeswax.

Dear, no. I saw the confirmation plain as day there in his face, the lady said. In any event, smells like someone around here's been eating onions recently. The Lord has blessed me with a powerful nose, can smell near on anything, and there's nothing worse than riding four hours on a bus with someone who's been eating onions. She opened her very tiny purse and took out a tin, pulled the top off, delicately lifted away the paper with the tip of her finger to reveal pale lozenges inside. Violet candy? she offered.

And, since Joanie and Buddy had both eaten onions on their burgers, they took one candy apiece.

Tastes like licking a plaster wall, Joanie said, making a face.

You're welcome. Took me a minute, but my perceptions about you sure did come clear at last, the lady said.

Oh, yeah? Joanie said.

Yes, I can see you're dumping your brother at that Farm Colony up in Gainesville, and going on alone to

Maine, 'cause you got you a job there. The lady squinted, looking at Joanie's shoes, her hands, her hair, her straw hat, and said, I don't know. Shopkeeper. No, no, I got it. Lady's companion.

Something struggled in Joanie, but at last she said with a smile she tried to bite down, Almost. Women's college.

College girl. Well, I'll be, the lady said. I myself begged and begged to go to college, but my daddy said no, not even a Christian college, not even a home economics course. Ada, honey, no amount of book reading can make a woman a better housekeeper, he always said to me. But of course that was a different time, before the first Great War, before women even got to vote and then got all uppity and started yelling for things. Well, to tell you the truth, I'm mighty envious of you going off to college. I would have loved to learn about the old books and philosophers and such. Though I say, I always do say, a woman's place is in the home. She said this with such vehemence, her chins wobbled.

One of the birds in the cage was sleeping, and the other was puffed up and preening under its wings. It stopped when it saw Buddy staring at it and shouted out, Red peril!

The lady laughed. Oh, it just tickles me no end

when he says that, she said. I taught him that myself. It's what all the boys used to call me back in the day, not because I'm one of them Communists, of course not, but because of my hair. She fluffed her hair with one plump hand and said, Red peril. I know you can't see it, but I used to be pretty as you, my girl.

I believe it if you say it, Joanie said. The bus had started moving through the long yellow afternoon, and the air blowing through the windows came as a great relief.

In any event, the lady said, college girl, let's see if you got the power of perception like me. Bet you can't take a look at me and tell my story the way I did with the bus driver and you.

All right, Joanie said, and she put on a very serious face and looked the woman over slowly and so hard that her eyes began to cross. At last, in a creepy voice, she said, You teach piano up in Gainesville. You come down here for a week every year to visit your sister but couldn't leave your birds behind because you're a spinster, and you live all alone in your little apartment up there. You and your sister don't get along at all, because of the bad blood between you. Your sister is still mad, deep down, that your daddy left the house up in town to you when he died and all she got was a bunch of fields full of nothing down in these parts. You spent the whole week playing solitaire in different rooms and quarreling over what you wanted to eat for supper.

The lady gaped at Joanie, her tiny eyes blinking fast. At last she said, Bless me. I'm a widow, not a spinster, but besides that, you're dead on. You're a natural, just like me.

Joanie laughed and said, Nah. My mama used to clean the house for your sister's neighbor, old Mr. Hubbard. Your sister would complain about your visits for weeks before you came down.

Oh, what a dirty trick! the lady cried out, her cheeks turning red. How un-Christian of you. But I don't know what I should have expected from a girl who is throwing away her own brother like he's trash. And then she turned her face indignantly toward the front of the bus and bellowed for all to hear, A friend loveth at all times, and a brother is born for adversity. Proverbs.

I'm seventeen, lady, Joanie said angrily. How the heck can I take care of a big old jug of molasses like him? Anyways, I was just having a little fun, Joanie said in a sweeter voice, but the lady had set her angry face toward her birds and her own window, where Florida was rushing by.

Joanie lowered her face to Buddy's shoulder and tried to muffle her laughter. Soon, though, she just rested her head there, and her eyes slowly closed and she fell asleep.

After some time, the lady with the birds extracted a peeled hard-boiled egg from her bag, opened a sheet of paper carefully, and dipped every bit of the white of the egg into the salt and pepper there. Buddy liked the way the lady ate the egg, in tiny fast bites, leaving the golden center for the end, which she rolled in the last of the salt and pepper and let sit in her mouth until it dissolved. Then she, too, fell asleep and her snores, high in her nose, rose up and down in the air of the bus.

Buddy liked everything about the bus right now: the feel of his sister's head on his shoulder and the smell of her hair; the way that the bumps in the road made the flesh of the woman with the birds jiggle; the way that the birds swayed inside the cage on their strange sharp feet and bobbed their pretty crests. Through the window, when he let his eyes unfocus, the desperate scrabbling cypresses with their feet in the water became a blur of gray and shining brown, and the palmettos spun a green weave. They stopped at each poky town along the way, but when the bus picked up speed again everything flashed gold and green and brown and blue, over and over, and the sun began to lower itself and upon his hands the hot yellow sunlight of late afternoon began to spread.

It was then that something caught Buddy's attention. Rather, it was the lack of something, for the bird lady's high snoring had stopped and a strange silence had overtaken the bus. He turned his head to look at the bird lady. She was wearing a serious face and leaning into the aisle. Now he saw that she was leaning over his sister's pocketbook, which, though the strap was still slung across her shoulder, had fallen off her lap and into the aisle. He saw the lady put her hand inside the pocketbook. Slowly, she pulled the roll of cash from it and held it in her hand, smiling. But then she looked up and saw Buddy watching her. Her face flushed and she blinked her eyes fast and licked her lips, then she peeled a bill away from the roll and shoved the rest back into the pocketbook, and closed the clasp with nimble fingers.

Just having a little joke, she whispered. Just some fun, no harm, she said, and tucked the bill she had taken down the neck of her blouse. She put a finger to her lips and went, Shush.

Joanie, Buddy said, shaking his sister.

Hush now, don't wake her, the lady said. Poor girl looks awful tired, she needs a rest. She took the paper bag of food that was squeezed between herself and the birdcage and tried to hand it to him. I got some nice ham sandwiches in there for you, she said, coaxingly. I don't even like ham, but my sister made me take them. There's some pecan sandies there, too. You like cookies? Everyone likes cookies.

Joanie, he said, but was distracted by the smell of the ham from the bag that the lady had dropped on his lap.

Anyways, the lady said, she won't miss it in the long run. Pretty girl like her can always find a way to make some money. She smiled, and there was lipstick all over her large front teeth.

Hey, Joanie, Buddy said with less conviction now, but his sister was sleeping hard and it took him a while to awaken her, and the bus was slowing, turning, and when she finally opened her eyes and wiped her mouth they had stopped at the station and he had forgotten what he wanted to tell her.

Before the bus even came to a halt, the bird lady had stood and pushed her way down the aisle with her cage and her suitcase so that she would be the first off, ahead of all the people who sat in the front of the bus.

LET ME TELL YOU, Joanie said, smoothing down her hair, which the air through the windows had ruffled, and looking at the lady who stood there so large at the front of the bus. Busybodies like that nasty old thing I certainly will not be missing up in Maine. From what I hear, them Yankees keep to themselves, as well they should.

They came off the bus into the long shadows of afternoon, the high spiky palm trees and the heritage oaks broad and dripping with moss. They took turns using the facilities at the bus station. While Buddy was waiting outside with the suitcases, and Joanie was inside the restroom, there came a terrible shriek and she ran out without even washing her hands. It's gone, she said. It's gone. I looked in my pocketbook for a comb and my hundred-dollar bill is gone. I'm never going to be able to buy my books and such now. And she sat down on her suitcase and screamed, low, into her hands.

Buddy sat beside her on his own suitcase and put his arm around her and began to cry, because he missed his mother so.

There were other people in the station walking around, but nobody bothered them. At last Joanie stopped screaming into her hands and got up and went back into the bathroom to wash her face, and when she came out she seemed somehow smaller and her face was blotchy but set.

What's that? she said, seeing the paper bag of food on his lap.

Bird lady give it to me, he said.

She opened the bag and whistled. Enough food here for days, she said. She looked at him. They'll be feeding you where you're going. Three square, they said. You mind if I take this, Bud? It'll feed me all the way until I get where I'm going, and she didn't wait to hear what he said, but just packed it into her suitcase.

Ham in there, he said sadly, his stomach feeling empty. And cookies.

We got about a mile to walk, she said. You still feeling pretty strong, Buddy?

Real strong, Buddy said, and took both of the suitcases and set off again, following his sister through the late afternoon.

Buddy liked the neighborhoods they were walking through, the big wooden houses with their porches, all the people out walking their dogs. There were young people, too, in twos and threes, and when Joanie watched them something that had died in her face back at the station came alive again. Bet they're students up at the university, she murmured. Bet they're out here because their brains are too stuffed with symphonies and history and classical Greek and they got to walk it all out to be able to sleep at night. And she smiled at Buddy and said kindly, In some ways, you're going off to your kind of college, too, I guess.

There was still light in the air when they crossed the

big road and saw the sign. The name change was so recent that the blasted old board with "Florida Farm Colony for Epileptic and Mentally Deficient Children" still hung on the left, while on the right there was a fresh-painted sign that said "Sunland."

Sunland, Joanie said, that's right, that's what they're calling it now. Doesn't that sound nice, Buddy? A land of sun.

That's where Mama's at, Joanie? Buddy said, and Joanie looked at him and her whole body started to shake. No, baby, she said, Mama's not there.

Then she said soft and fast to herself, Oh, my god, what am I doing? What am I doing? Mama always said she had me to take care of you in case something happened to her, and look what I'm doing.

But Buddy had turned eagerly toward the place, and was now walking fast up to the gate where the guard was snoozing in his hut, a transistor radio playing beside him. Wait, Buddy, Joanie called out behind him.

You must be Robert, ain't you, boy? the guard said. I was beginning to despair for you. They said you was coming today, but it's near time to lock the gates. And here you are.

Here I am, Buddy said. I'm Buddy.

Fifteen more minutes and you woulda had to find a

place to stay for the night, come back in the morning, the guard said to Joanie.

I'm sorry, sir, she said. She was pale all over, even in her lips.

The guard spoke into his walkie-talkie, and a garbled sound came back out.

Through the gate they could see straight lines of sago palms and oleanders, lights on in the windows of the great plain white wooden buildings scattered around on the sparse grass. Buddy grasped the gate and pressed his face painfully between the metal bars to look harder. One of the doors of the closest building opened and out of it three figures in white appeared and began to descend the stairs, shining backlit in the warm light that poured out from inside and painted the grass and the trees framing the building with gold.

Oh, Buddy breathed, because the sight was beautiful to him.

Bud, listen to me, Joanie said quickly beside him. I'll come back for you. I'll get my education, then I'll get my job, and when I have enough money to support us both I'll come back to get you. Oh, Lord, forgive me.

But Buddy wasn't listening. He was watching the three stout women in white coming closer to him across the path. From this distance he couldn't see their faces.

Any one of them could be his mama. The early moon hung in the blue of the end of the day above, and in the distance, a cat darted swiftly across the grounds, and Joanie, who smelled like sweat and onions and like herself, rose up on her toes and kissed his cheek. The evening breeze lifted from across the farm fields with its warm smell of cows and dirt and touched him on his face and hands and neck, and in the smell there was something wilder, something off the wet and teeming prairie a few miles away, with its dark, terrible beasts below the water, the delicate angelic birds on their long, thin legs above. In this moment, the voice inside him that was always singing, that nobody else could hear, sang louder, sang until the women came so close that at last they showed their faces. Then Joanie, whom he blinked at, trying to understand, turned her own face from him and began to walk away, fast, and did not look back.

Brawler

Sara came into the blaze late, the boys already leaping froglike across the deck, the girls gone bald in silicone caps. In the afternoon sunlight the pool was harsh; she'd left it only this morning in the soft plum dawn.

The other team was lined up around the eastern gutter, doing its cheer, a slow solemn clapping that built into syncopated yips and the pounding of feet on metal. The noise made pocks of confusion across the surface of the water.

THE DIVING COACH TURNED to see her coming across the wet deck. You're late, he yelled over the other team's noise, but he looked relieved. She shrugged, and took off her anorak to begin her stretching, but he grabbed her hand and lifted it to examine the bloodied knuckles. Brawler, he said. The other girls told me what happened and I didn't think they'd let you out. She took her hand away. She didn't tell him that they had not in fact let her out; that when the detention aide had fallen asleep she'd opened a window silently at the back of the room, pushed her backpack out, swung her body over the lip, pulled the window shut with one hand, and hung on the exterior sill for a moment before falling into the fresh pine mulch ten feet below. It was not nearly as soft as water.

THE MORE NERVOUS or show-offy divers climbed and dived, climbed and dived, like good little penguins, but she stayed on the deck loosening up and watching the first races, giving a small jump each time the buzzer cracked and the swimmers leapt off the blocks. She loved the churn and the separation of bodies as the slower swimmers fell behind the swifter. Sometimes they let her swim a sprint relay; she was wickedly fast, but in races she forgot to breathe and couldn't go farther than fifty meters before having to stop. Also, she was no longer a swimmer, not for a year, since she had been discovered to be brushing the boys' junk in their Speedos with her hand as they swam by in the next lane at practice. Most of the boys hadn't complained, some had even slowed down as they passed, but it took only one whiner, and then she was forced to switch to diving, which was where she should have been all along anyway.

There was a coldness on her shoulder that slid down her chest, the coach quietly giving her a lime sports drink. She drank it down in one draught; it was a hot day and she had walked all the way from the school. *Need a snack?* he said softly, and though she hadn't yet eaten today she said no, because hunger made her feel cleaner. The other girls didn't like the coach because he wore such short shorts that when he sat in his rusty chair to watch them dive his purplish balls spilled out the leg hole. She liked him, though. He was kind to her, fed her, kept the other girls off her back, which of course made them like her even less. She didn't care. The other girls barely mattered.

At last the waves in the lap pool smoothed out and it was time for the diving. She didn't watch the other divers; she didn't need to. She just breathed and imagined herself held gently within each of her dives.

And then they called her name and she stood slowly and came to the ladder. As she climbed, the person she was, that skinny slinking girl with the bad skin and teeth, fell away. Her nerves clenched inward and there rose up an internal hum that blocked out the voices of the people in the stands and the water lipping at the gutters and the sun itself, and, at last, her own body. At the top she was a pinprick in nothing. She edged backward to the end of the springboard and all of her muscles bunched, ready, buzzing; she raised her arms and gave two giant jumps, then breathed out with the third and lifted herself into the broad air, and there was the delicious pause at the top as she was already in the first backward somersault, so perfect she could stay floating here forever; and even this was not nearly as beautiful as the next part, the falling into the second somersault, which shattered the world into a billion bright and jagged shards flung outward from her spinning body. Now her hands knifed into the water, her body threading after, and there was no splash, she could feel the downward gulp of the water. She gathered herself for a moment under the blue, then surfaced. The coach was in midair, leaping; then noise returned, her teammates, the other divers, the adults in the stands shouting, and they were shouting for her. She pulled her body up and away from the pool. And it was then that she felt the sting on the back of her neck, the fine rip in the skin where it had just brushed the board, and before the judges saw it and disqualified her she touched it quickly with her split and bloodied knuckles to hide the fact that it was this newer wound that bled a watery red stripe down her back.

IT WAS TWILIGHT and the boy was dreaming of smooth gray shifting shapes that emerged from the fog and dissolved to nothing again. He blinked and saw Sara standing on the other side of the glass door just before she opened it, first sliding her hand in and holding the strand of bells hanging from the frame, then bringing the rest of her body silently inside. Her pale face was a question. He looked at the office and turned back to give her a nod. Then she went quickly to the freezer in the rear of the store and put two frozen dinners into her backpack, and was already at the front, leaning her wet hair into the ice cream cooler, when the boy's mother came rushing out of the back, talking at him, telling him in her language to keep his eye on this thieving sneaky little bitch. Yes, Mother, he said to her. Sara came up out of the ice cream case with a mango Popsicle and flushed cheeks, and put two quarters near the register, sliding them to the boy. He looked at her hand, the tape with its browning spots of blood, curling at the edges from the wet of the pool. He had heard about the fight, the boy in fifth period, her swift snapping. You win? he said. She looked at her hand also and said quietly, Always. He said, No, not the fight, I meant the diving. That's what I meant, too, she said and half smiled, then waved the Popsicle at the woman, who quivered beside her son, and went into the twilight again.

She walked up the street, her steps growing slower as she came closer to home. There were no basements in this town with its fragile bedrock, but the apartment block was built into a hill, and she lived in the cheapest unit, which was half-underground. She entered the linoleum-floored front hall of the building, turned the corner, and went down the stairwell toward her door. During construction, someone had had the idea to filter the hallway light into her dim living room through a series of four colored windows above the banister, and so as the girl descended she could look inside and see the lump of her mother on the couch lit by the shivering television glow, in red, then orange, then blue, and finally green. Even through the door she could hear the mechanical hum and over it the sound of the program, a man's voice narrating something infinitely wearisome. She held the Popsicle's wrapper between her teeth, took her shoes off and left them outside, put her slippers on, and unlocked the door.

The smell crashed into her, sweet rot and her mother's eucalyptus rub. The dehumidifiers were on, the air conditioners in the windows were on, and even the ozone generator, which the girl felt sure was slowly poisoning her, was on. She turned all the machines off, save for one air conditioner, and in the new quiet the television narrator's voice was painfully loud. A cheetah chased across the screen in gorgeous slow motion. She turned the volume down to a murmur. Her mother's eyes were closed, and she was in her white cotton pajamas, with her white cotton sheet and pillow covering the couch, keeping her from contaminants. The goblet of pills she was supposed to have taken that morning stood on the coffee table, beside the glass of vodka she used to wash them down, but neither had been touched. Her mother drank nothing but vodka now; it killed the germs, she said. She no longer trusted water, certainly not tap, which had lead and fluoride and bacteria in it, but not bottled, either; who knew where bottled water came from? All she ate were her pills and sometimes a Popsicle, but only mango. Mango, she said, is the cleanest kind of fruit.

Mom, Sara said, but her mother only moaned and opened her eyes, then closed them again. Sara took the Popsicle out of the wrapper and put it to her mother's dry lips. She breathed a curl of frosty vapor off the Popsicle, but turned her head away from the taste.

Months ago, her mother had passed out, freeing

Sara to call an ambulance. They had spent all night in the ER, the girl insisting on test after test until there were no more tests to take and her mother wept weakly and begged to go home. In the morning, the young doctor at the end of his shift looked at the girl's devastated face in the waiting room, and while the nurses were helping Sara's mother to get dressed he took her to get a hot chocolate from the cafeteria and then showed her the meditation room. They raked the sand in a tabletop Zen garden side by side for a while until at last Sara said, So, what's wrong with her?

And the doctor said, carefully, Hard to say. How long has this been going on?

I don't know, Sara said. It's always changing. It was cell phones at first, then it was mold, now it's something else, extreme sensitivity to a bunch of things. It's a mixture, I think.

Huh, the doctor said. And she's not eating?

She can't, Sara said. She takes eighty-something pills a day and they fill her up.

But they're not prescribed? the doctor said.

Oh, yes, they are, Sara said. She has a naturopath and a homeopath and a Chinese-medicine lady, too.

Ah, the doctor said. But none of these people are making it better?

No, the girl said. Actually, she keeps getting worse. She's real skinny.

Yes, the doctor said slowly, she's malnourished. And she was dehydrated when she got here.

Sara listened hard, but there was no judgment in the doctor's voice, so she said, Can you make her stay?

The doctor rubbed his tired face. Oh, honey, he said. Not until she makes an attempt to hurt herself or someone else.

But she is hurting herself, Sara said. Or someone else. That's exactly what she's doing.

But not to the point of hospitalization yet. It's delicate, the doctor said.

Then they were silent until Sara put down the little rake and, looking away from the doctor, said so quickly that she seemed angry, But maybe she's not sick? Maybe she's just pretending? And the doctor regarded her fully and his eyes felt so heavy on her face that she glanced up at him and saw his thick black eyebrows that bunched behind his glasses and the kindness there, and these things together, absurdly, made her want to kiss him.

Listen, he said. We don't know what's causing your mother's pain. But you need to know that wherever it comes from, whether from her body or from her brain, it is real.

OK, she said. But that was the moment when she knew he would lie to her, and everything in her spun away from him, and he was the one she hated as she walked out the door.

Now Sara put the Popsicle gently on the plate beneath the full goblet of pills, and went to the bathroom to shower and change into her own bleached white pajamas. Her mother insisted that both bleach and white fabric kept the germs of the outside world away.

The bathroom was luxurious, the best place in the apartment, gray-veined white marble; her father had redone it with tiles he'd taken from a construction job a long time ago. Somewhere in the heap of things beside the television was a tape Sara's parents had made of her as a baby swimming happily in the claw-foot tub, sleek and fat and shining, before she could even crawl. But this was all she knew of her father—he was long gone—and the bathroom had become her own place, her mother barely visiting it.

Tonight, Sara didn't want to leave it, she wanted to fill the tub and soak herself in heat, but she forced herself to come out into the living room again. On the television was a family of elephants in the glossy mud, flapping their ears against the flies and spraying water on their backs. The narrator was saying portentously, "Elephants keep cool on a blazing day." Her mother hadn't shifted, but her ribs moved shallowly with her breath.

Sara took the frozen dinners from her backpack, slit the plastic, put them both in the microwave, and watched them spin for eight minutes. Then she took them steaming in the dish towel to the couch.

Her mother smelled the food and groaned, then her eyes opened and she whispered, Baby. She moved her feet painfully to make room for her daughter, then thought better of it and said, Help? She no longer owned consonants, only soft vowels. The girl put her food on the floor, and lifted her mother. She was a skin bag with chalk in it, far too light to be human. Sara took her to the bathroom, and held her over the toilet, and gave her the paper and pulled up her underwear and took her back to the couch. This time, she laid her mother down in the opposite direction so that her mother's head was in her lap. Sara set her food on the armrest, so that if she spilled it she wouldn't burn her mother's papery skin. She ate without tasting, which may have been a blessing: The food was just hot brown in brown sauce. She finished, and put her hand on her mother's cool head.

On the television, the elephants transformed into lions and lions transformed into great huffing buffalo. The night went full black in the apartment's windows.

As a male springbok climbed aboard a female springbok, and the narrator's voice grew husky with excitement, Sara became aware of a deeper and stranger silence underlying the murky underworld of the apartment, something like darkness throbbing in the places where the television's light didn't reach. She held her breath and heard only the air conditioner, the narrator, her own heart in her ears. And then all at once she felt it, a slippage, a slickness, and even though it wasn't taking place within her own body, she could see the slow and uncontrollable dilation downward and outward, into a vast sun-bright plain full of golden grasses swaying as though brushed by a great hand, and a horizon that didn't stop in the vagueness that came at the end of sight, but pressed on into the palest and most fragmented of blues.

For a long time, Sara did not move. She held her body tightly within its stillness as her mother's ear pressed heavy, cooling, into the flesh of her leg. Sara was frozen within time even as the television scrolled onward through the miracles of the savanna and the lifting of white names through blackness, then the program leapt a continent into the icy reaches of the north, with its glaciers like green inverse cathedrals and its savage dark beasts swimming in the waters beneath.

She kept herself still and ached, and yet forced more stillness upon herself, because she knew that the moment her body weakened and moved despite her ferocious will, that movement would reawaken time; and it would all catch up to her in a bound, and the terrible thing now happening would have to be reckoned with, the future rising and rising ever upward, and she would be drawn into the denser and darker and far lonelier stuff that would make up the rest of her life.

Birdie

The women were drinking peach schnapps, telling stories about the worst things they'd ever done. They had already skimmed through the missing years with haste, as though the past were gruesome, the two decades of lost friendship something untouchable and rotten. Maybe it was, Nic thought. Melodie had said she was a Realtor in San Luis Obispo, still playing the field. Her face was so artificially plumped and frozen that it resembled a Greek chorus mask that slid between genres and settled on tragicomedy. Sammie was overripe, a bruised apple. Five kids with Hank, she had said with a sigh, all seven of them packed into the little house her mother had left her, in the same little town where the women had all grown up. Birdie was dying, the reason why they'd all been summoned. She had only her friends and her parents these days, because she had been a freelancer and had worked alone, and her boyfriend had taken off at the first diagnosis, stealing the cat. Only Nic was the same as she'd been when they knew her, just a tad more droopy and wrinkled now—a law professor, one kid, divorce, chunky jewelry, the whole shebang. In this room, she was hyperaware of how boring her life was, but also that she was the one who was clearly managing the best. A surprise, fortune favoring the brittle.

Snow hissed against the window. The hospital moved in its mechanical intricacy behind the door. The three old friends were perched near Birdie, who lay pale and skinny from the neck down, though her face was unreal in its puffiness, as if covered by a floppy creature sucking on the bones of her skull. Only those darting blue-black eyes were hers.

Melodie was now saying that the worst thing she had ever done was at an awful party she was catering in the Hills, just after some bigwig cornered her in the pantry and touched her under her skirt. I threw a bottle of olive oil at his head and came crashing out into the dining room, she said. And then I realized I no longer had to take any of this shit, and that I was done trying to charm this room full of rich people, and for what? A nonspeaking part in a movie never released in theaters and a cruddy efficiency with a rodent problem way out in Encino? No thank you. So I stole a twenty-thousand-dollar mink out of the coatroom and took off. I don't even feel bad because I'm like, if you have twenty thousand dollars to park in a coatroom, you have twenty thousand dollars to throw away on me. And I still have it in my closet. I mean, it's ugly as sin. But sometimes when I'm sad I get naked and wear it fur-side in, and I feel at peace with my life decisions for like a hot minute.

They laughed, and then Sammie said in a sort of fast whisper that her worst thing ever was terrible and they were all going to hate her if she said it. And when they said, No, no, Sammie, come on, she got tears in her eyes and said quaveringly that she'd had an abortion.

That's your worst thing ever? Melodie said. Christ, Sammie, I've had two abortions and feel great about them. We don't need to let men spawn in our bodies.

I've had one, too, Birdie said. A quarter of women in this country have them. Abortion's morally neutral, I think.

I've had three, said Nic, who hadn't had even one, but solidarity seemed the right call in this scenario.

Always one-upping us, Nichole, Melodie said with a smile that, on her frozen face, was all teeth.

A series of emotions passed over Sammie's face, but

at last she settled into a large tight solemnity and they could see her judging them from behind it. Then the women were all looking at Nic, so she took a swig of schnapps and steeled herself and said, The worst thing I ever did was, I guess, what happened that summer just after we graduated, right before we all left home. I was babysitting for a couple who lived out on the lake about six miles north of town. They worked at the opera. He was a set designer and she did costumes.

And she was about to go into the whole story—the delicious old winterized camp that was painted a green-black, and its crisp white modern interior, the husband and wife like sleek seals, the toddler she loved like her own child, who slept with his hands curled near his ears—when she saw the other three exchanging looks and repressing their smiles, and that old whip of their judgment snapped out of the darkness of time and stung her. Nic cried out, What? What?

Oh my god, Melodie said. We were right. We totally knew it. We totally knew you were having an affair with the boy's father.

That's actually why we stopped talking to you, Sammie said. We were so mad at you! You sexy little home-wrecker! Ha ha ha ha ha ha ha ha ha ha.

Birdie put her swollen dry hand on Nic's and said, I am sorry about the way we treated you. You were just a kid, not even eighteen. And we were so cruel to you that summer. We're so sorry.

You were cruel to me? Nic said. I had no idea. I just thought we were all busy that summer and couldn't hang out.

There was a long pause, then Melodie said, Well, I mean, we three hung out. We just never called you. You were kind of persona non grata. We called you Nic-hole.

Yikes, Nic said. Wow.

I mean, in our defense, kids are pretty morally rigid, you know? Sammie said. I mean it wasn't right what you did or anything but we definitely should have been nicer to you or like made some kind of attempt to understand or whatever. I mean, my oldest is only a few years away from that age, and I don't know but I'm pretty sure she's having sex? Probably not with married men, but who knows anymore? She doesn't tell me anything and these kids all have this whole separate life online nowadays. Oh god! she cried, and looked off into the distance, blinking.

Nic tried to remember feeling left out and lonely that summer, but all that returned to her now was a kind of fullness, a warmth and smoothness and a sharpening of all the beauty that had surrounded her until it was so intense that she could hardly recognize anything beyond the confines of her own body. That summer still dazzled her with its light. She hadn't even noticed her friends ignoring her; she had been too happy within herself.

In any case, we're sorry, Birdie said. Her breathing had tightened and her eyes had narrowed to slits; she was clearly in pain, and she fumbled for and pressed a button with urgency. They all watched, helpless before the enormity of their old friend's suffering, but soon the drugs washed into Birdie and soothed her and she smiled again.

Anyway, the worst thing I ever did is something I think about all the time, Birdie said. This is why I asked the question. I was in middle school and there was this friend of mine who would come over to my house to escape a pretty awful situation at home.

There was a lot of that in our town, Melodie said. An entire town made out of bad situations.

Still is, Sammie said. The stories I could tell! Just give me another drink and I will, she said, and she gulped the schnapps and coughed, but before she could give them the gossip, Birdie said quickly, Anyway, I both liked and didn't like this kid. There was this extreme sweetness but also such awkwardness it made me want to run away or cringe or lock the door and pretend not to be home whenever I saw my friend walking up the hill to my house. And my parents were really religious but good people and they kind of knew what was going on at my friend's house and though they were super-strict usually, they let us have all the sleepovers we wanted. So, at one point my friend turned to me and I was given this pretty heavy secret. And I kept it for a while, like a year or so, but then one night, out of some kind of irritation—I think I had wanted to go to someone else's house for a birthday party but couldn't because I had to have a sleepover with this little hanger-on who just seemed so drippy and lame that night—I became furious. So I got up in the middle of the night and wrote an anonymous letter to my friend's parents and told them everything that I knew about their daughter. And the punishment was severe, like, the parents would be called by DHS nowadays it was so bad, and after that there were no more sleepovers, not for a long time. And the worst part was that my friend never even blamed me for it, but I saw some of the light inside had dimmed. I knew that I was the one who had done it. And you can't get that innocence back. Once it's gone, it's gone. And I couldn't forgive myself. I still haven't, she said. Her mouth had gone dry and was making clicking noises.

Oh, you need to forgive yourself, Sammie said gravely. Holding grudges is where cancer comes from.

They all looked at Sammie, who seemed confused at the sudden attention; the wind shrieked gently against the side of the building. At last, the door opened and a doctor stepped in. He was good-looking in a wispy middle-aged runner kind of way, and Melodie's face became alert.

What do we have here? he said. Birdie's bevy?

The cancer cabal, Nic said, and the doctor flicked his eyes at her in recognition, another joker in the room.

Birdie introduced each woman and said, In high school, we called ourselves the E's. Our names all end in -ie.

The doctor looked at Nic and said, But not Nic, and she said, Nope. They tried to call me Nickie but I would never answer to it, and they finally gave up.

So, Nic and the E's, he said. A bad cover band. Nice to meet you. I regret to tell you, he said, putting his hand on Birdie's shoulder, it is time to say good night. Birdie needs her rest. You all can come back to visit in the morning. Nine a.m. sharp.

The women stood, feeling unbalanced, and one by one they kissed Birdie's swollen cheek, unconsciously holding their breath as though not to take her pain into their bodies. They grabbed their roller bags from where they'd parked them in the corner and fled the room.

There was more air in the hallway, or they could breathe now, and they relaxed a little as they walked. I took a cab here, said Melodie. Me too, said Sammie. Nic sighed internally and said, I rented a car. I'll drive us to the hotel. But in the hospital's lobby, they stopped to look out the great windows into the wildness of wind and snow and it seemed so astonishingly huge and fearsome, some dark beast roaring at them, that nobody moved until Nic at last said, I'll go out and get the car and pull it up here for you, and both of the other women said, Great, thanks!

Nic felt a shock of pain in immersing herself in such cold. Then again, after seeing Birdie in her bed, it seemed right to be scoured by ice and darkness, to be stripped back to the animal body. Nic wanted to cry, and obligingly the wind bit at her eyes and made them water, then froze the tears to the corners of her eyes. The rental car smelled like plastic and sadness, and she put the heat on full blast and drove back to the entrance where the women were waiting in the warmth and light. They threw their bags into the trunk and climbed in, shivering, and Nic moved slowly through the parking lot and out onto the highway, filled with snowbanks and the brave red taillights of other cars barely visible before her. Where the tires had worn the ice down to the black asphalt, the wind of the passing cars was blowing snow in writhing snakes that the headlights caught and made glow golden. It was hypnotic to watch. The other two women were talking, but Nic was driving carefully and didn't listen until at last Melodie turned to her and said, You're awfully quiet, Nichole. Ignoring us?

Just trying to keep us alive, she said.

Is that some kind of joke? Sammie said. Because Birdie is dying? Because if it is, it isn't funny.

No, I'm literally trying to keep the wind from swerving us into a semitruck in this miserable fucking blizzard, Sammie, Nichole said.

Oh, Sammie said, and started to weep. Sorry. I'm just really on edge all the time these days. I can't even tell you how much I needed this weekend. The two other women tried not to smile at this, until Melodie gave up and snorted, and Sammie said defensively, Wait, I know how that sounded and it wasn't what I meant, I know this isn't like a girls' weekend at a spa or whatever, but you try having five children.

Never, said Melodie. Kill me first.

One child sometimes seems too much for me, Nic said, and thought of her weird little girl a thousand miles away, falling asleep right now to whale song. Instead of being with her, Nic had chosen to be here, handmaiden to death, reliving middle school with these so-called friends of hers she wasn't sure she'd liked even in their heyday. Birdie had been the good queen to Melodie's wicked one, Sammie had been the rook, stout and square and locked into her rigid right angles, and what was Nic? The knight. Leaping over you in panic, slaying from the side. There had been no pawns; or rather the entire rest of the world had been pawns, disposable and in the way. Why was she making chess metaphors? She hadn't played chess in decades. She had never felt more exhausted in her life.

At last, the lights of their hotel slid up the windshield, and they parked as closely to the glowing glass doors as they could. They dragged their bags through the snow and inside. There were fresh hot cookies at the hotel desk and while they waited, Sammie took three. Meet in my room at seven for drinks, ladies! she said at the elevator through a mouthful of cookie, but Nic begged off, saying she would have to call her daughter, though this was a lie. Her daughter was already dreaming, far away.

For a long time, she sat on the side of the bed in the hotel robe, weary, bathing in the light of home renovation shows on the television. She called down to reception for food service, but the nice girl named

Dagmar, who'd checked them in, laughed at her. What you take this place for, the Ritz? she said. No food service. Is the restaurant, pizza delivery. But through this big storm, eh, she said doubtfully.

Dagmar, Nic said, if I have to spend any more time with the women I came with, I will go absolutely bonkers.

Understand, Dagmar said. Blond one is in the bar talking now to the businessmen and drinking pink wine. And, oof, now here comes pretty one out of elevator.

Pretty one? said Nic.

No, correct, not pretty, Dagmar said diplomatically. Sexy one. I do not understand these fat lips. Like a duck, no? How to speak with duck lips?

Oh, they're not made like that for talking, Nic said.

They laughed, and then Dagmar said, Listen, they sit now beyond the bar, you sneak in on other side, you sit far from your friends, in shadows behind a wall. Is all I can say.

Is good. Is a lot, said Nic, and thanked her and hung up.

Nic dressed again in all black, like a ninja, and pulled her hair back severely, and hoped that this would be enough to hide her from the others. She slipped in the way that Dagmar had told her and hid behind the menu and when Dagmar came over from the desk to take her order, the girl laughed at her. You look like spy, the girl said.

You have to be a waitress, too, Dagmar? You're a woman of great capabilities, Nic said.

Is only three workers who come in the storm. We share jobs, Dagmar said with a shrug. She had applied a pale pink lip gloss that made her mouth seem almost unseemly in its wetness. Nic looked away. Just give me your cheapest bottle of red wine and your fastest meal to go, she said, and the girl, deflated, sped off.

As Nic waited, she could hear the voices of Melodie and Sammie talking on the other side of the bar, but not their words, until the four businessmen who'd been chatting and watching a game stood and threw down their money and went back up to their rooms. Now there were only a few people left in the bar, all loners, and the women's voices came clear.

I'm like really worried about her, Sammie was saying in a voice blurry with alcohol. She seems bad. Like, poor thing!

And Nic smiled, because a person dying of cancer could certainly be called a poor thing.

Right? She seems so unhappy that it just like radiates off her, Melodie said. She was never so dour and grim and like jumpy when we were young, right? She was the kind of kid who was always telling goofy jokes and doing things to make other people happy. I was so jealous of how she got all the good parts in the plays! And she didn't even want to be an actress, I did. How bad must her life be to like emanate such hatred toward everyone.

Thank goodness she at least has her daughter, Sammie said; and this is how Nic knew for sure they weren't talking about Birdie. They were talking about her.

One of the men at the bar took his gently chiming bourbon over to the women, and said, Ladies, would you mind terribly if I bought you a drink, and Sammie's giggle was so delighted, Nic could see how her night would unroll, how starved she was for exactly this kind of adventure.

Nic grabbed the soup and wine that Dagmar held out to her, signed the room charge slip with a ludicrous tip for the girl, and scuttled off, her heart going fast in her rage. Her life was unhappy? The other two were so desperate for love that one mutilated her face and the other couldn't stop pumping out babies. Back in the room, she burned her tongue on Dagmar's soup, and finally the tears that had been frozen behind her eyes all day thawed and were released and she cried and cried for her poor burnt tongue, for her poor lost youth, for poor Birdie who had once been so pale and tall and slender and redheaded she'd reminded Nic of a lit candle.

Just before nine, as she was drifting off to sleep, the hotel phone rang, and Nic picked it up, thinking of her daughter, catastrophe, a house on fire, but it was Dagmar. A little pulse stirred in Nic's gut, then Dagmar said, Your friends, they make me call, she said. They say, Ask if is all right? So I ask.

My best friend is days from death, I'm stuck in a midrange hotel in a blizzard, hiding from the two biggest bitches known to man, and I've already seen this home renovation show, so obviously I've never been better, Nic said.

She heard Dagmar say, Being sarcastic, seems fine. They say meet for breakfast at eight in the a.m. Dagmar hung up.

Sleep came crashing down on Nic, and she woke with a dry mouth at six to find that the wind had abated and the sky was going pink over a field swept white with fresh whipped snow. She considered going to the gym, but was sure she'd find Melodie there, refining the beautiful muscles of her body. Instead she lay in the clean giant bed, luxuriating in the silence and calm. Her daughter would have been awake for an hour already, and would now be tapping Nic's face or making the music robot play that same damn song about sharks that all the children were obsessed with and dancing around the room, saying, I'm starving! Feed me! until Nic got up and made her eggs.

She watched the clock slip forward until she was afraid she wasn't ever going to get up. But at the last minute she took a swift shower and packed her things, and was at the wan buffet of hard-boiled eggs and assorted packaged carbohydrates before the other two women. She drank a coffee and ate an apple with peanut butter. Dagmar had been replaced by a stout man with a busy expression, and Nic laughed at herself for feeling disappointed at not seeing the girl again. The elevator opened to Melodie, her makeup perfect, moving in a haze of perfume so strong that Nic's eyes watered. She looked at the buffet with a frown and took a black coffee, and sat down opposite Nic. But instead of saying something mean, which the old Melodie would have done, she put her hand on the table palm-side up, and looked at Nic until Nic put her own hand in hers. At the touch, Melodie's eyes filled with tears that slowly fell down the taut skin of her face, and Nic lost her appetite, and closed her own eyes and breathed. When she opened them, Sammie had joined them, and was eating a bowl of sugar cereal, her eyes darting back and forth between the other women's faces.

Melodie blotted her cheeks with a napkin and sighed, then squinted at Sammie and said, Is that a hickey?

Sammie turned a lurid pink and said, No! but Melodie had already unzipped her makeup case from her bag and was dabbing the bruise with a wand of concealer.

Don't tell, Sammie said. Oh my gosh, you can't tell. It's just that. I just needed something. I just needed something, anything else in my goddamn little old life.

What is there to tell? Nic said. Your neck ran into a doorknob.

Plus, you know, your body, your choice, Melodie said.

You two are such jerks, Sammie said with admiration.

THE HIGHWAYS WERE SWEPT and clear of cars, and they were so early for visiting hours that they went to the cafeteria and got more coffee, which was surprisingly good. When they went up to Birdie's floor, Birdie looked worse, and if Nic were a superstitious woman, she might have said that behind Birdie's shoulder, death had taken another vulture step nearer, was breathing on her.

The doctor came by briefly and squeezed Nic's shoulder as he left them for his other patients. Melodie had clocked the gesture and grimaced, but Nic would have given him to Melodie if she could; she had no need for a moderately good-looking doctor a thousand miles away from her life. They chatted about nothing, about people from the town who had ceased to be real to most of them decades ago, and Sammie glowed as she spoke, and Melodie painted Birdie's nails a color she called Whore Red.

At last, it was time for the others to leave. Nic could have gone to the airport a few hours early to deliver the other two in time for their flights, but she was finished—finally, for good—with trying to please people she didn't care about, and she said maybe it would be best if the other two shared a cab. Sammie hugged them all, and sat with Birdie and kissed her temple and whispered something long and fervent, weeping. Melodie squeezed Birdie's hands, and when she turned to Nic, she said, in a quick low tone, If we both keep mellowing out, I think we'll be the best of friends when we're ninety.

Oh good, Nic said, let's make plans to meet up then.

Melodie barked a laugh and hugged Nic, forcing her perfume into her nose, and said, Don't worry, I see through all the crustiness. I know you're a softy deep down. And then the women were gone.

Alone now, Nic and Birdie smiled at each other, and then Nic kicked off her shoes and put her head on Birdie's pillow and lay down next to her friend.

All those years lay between them, the lost years when they spoke on the phone only twice a month; the other years shot through with blazing intensity. Though their bodies were touching, there was no way to leap back to the other side.

I realized, Birdie said, we never actually let you tell your story yesterday.

No, Nic laughed. Your version was kind of imposed on me.

I've been thinking all night about your story. It didn't happen the way we thought it did, did it? Birdie said. I could tell when you started to wear that sly look of yours. You were going to let us live with the wrong idea.

I guess I realized I didn't want Melodie or Sammie to have it, Nic said. It felt too precious to give to them.

But to me? Birdie said.

You know I'd give you anything, Nic said.

Please do, said Birdie.

Nic took a deep breath, and she told Birdie the long version of the story, parceling out all the details that she'd so savored these years.

SHE HAD MET RICHARD and Deanna at the farmers market the weekend after she'd graduated from high school, she told Birdie. She was selling her father's flowers. Gladioluses, that week. Red and yellow and pink. They've always seemed wildly sexual, nearly embarrassing, since then.

Then the couple walked in, and they were unmistakably alien, shining and beautiful, both dark, both sleek, in sunglasses, which in that town was seen as an affectation. They held the hands of their boy between them, swinging him, and he laughed, slightly hysterical, and already without knowing him, Nic loved him for his sweetness, his sharp little face. She crouched and handed him the tip of a yellow gladiolus that had broken off, and he took it with a scream of delight, and when she stood again, the parents had taken off their sunglasses and were looking at her. She had never been looked at so minutely or with such interest. Later, she understood that they looked at all the world as though they were eating it up and it was the most delicious thing they'd ever tasted—that it wasn't just her, that they were interested in everything, they were artists—but at the time she felt all parts of her body tingling. They were in town for the summer for the festival up at the opera house, they said. They were looking for a babysitter.

Well, that's interesting, she said, I'm looking for a job, and she felt her blush rising hot out of the neck of her T-shirt, up her jawline, into her cheeks. She already had lined up a job at a baseball cap store, but it was minimum wage and not the kind of thing she felt, even then, was worthy of her. They looked delighted and said they would give her ten dollars an hour, which was twice her normal babysitting rate, and for only one boy. She scrawled her address and phone number on a slip of newspaper, and they said they would pick her up on Monday morning at eight.

This was the dawn of the internet, and so after the farmers market closed and her father picked up the money and the leftover flowers, she went to the computers in the library and looked the couple up. It wasn't like today, when the web sends its endless tentacles into our lives. Back then online information was scarce, but she did discover that both were well-known in their fields, and she printed out blurry photos of them and kept them in her nightstand at home. She didn't sleep at all that Sunday night and was enervated and anxious at dawn.

When the car came up the lane, it was a gray Jaguar, so beautiful she felt unworthy of riding in it. Richard was smiling at her in his glasses, dressed in a tight navy polo shirt that surprised her; it seemed so preppy for an artist to be wearing. They loved this area, he said. They'd been coming since college, and just last year had bought an old wreck of a camp and hired men to fix it up over the winter. This was their first summer living there, and so far, only three days in, they adored it.

The old camp was a stunning hunter green in morning light and black in the shadows of the afternoon, set on a small peninsula so that views of the lake filled three windows. She felt from inside as though she were standing in water. Their aesthetic was radical simplicity, so they had kept the wooden interior, but painted it white and removed walls, opening it up into a great, vaulted downstairs room with a kitchen, bathroom, and primary bedroom beneath the upstairs, where the boy's room, a bathroom, and a guest room were.

She had never before been in a place where every detail had been carefully selected, from the blown-glass light fixtures, to the handmade wrought iron cabinet pulls, to the walnut furniture her parents would have called ugly, but that looked ravishingly sculptural to her on the bare wooden floors. When she walked in that first time, she felt the way she'd felt when she was little and walked into church on Sunday, before her logic caught up with god. Deanna hugged her, smelling like lotion and the lake from her morning swim. She was in a sheer black linen dress, and had saved cinnamon pancakes for Nic, apologizing for the early hour. The boy climbed into Nic's lap as though she was his old friend. Deanna had written out the boy's schedule and given her the keys to the Volvo. Then the couple kissed their boy and left together in the Jaguar. Nic was so happy to be in this house, with its delicious food, its cleanliness and quiet and books, to have the lake to explore all day.

As the day passed, she began to feel a bit strange there alone with the boy in the house. It was as if she were two people: the almost-eighteen-year-old misfit ready to leave this tiny place yet frightened of the world, and at the same time her future self, living her own ideal life, in this quiet and peace with her child and her beautiful things all around her. In the future place, people asked her about her feelings and treated each other with gentleness, and there was no sudden danger, no violence, no sharpness.

On good days, Nic said now to Birdie, whose eyes were blinking rapidly in her swollen face, my life is not that far from this early vision of it. It's funny that even then, I didn't see a partner in the picture, she said, laughing. Birdie pressed her hand and she went on.

At the end of the first week, Richard drove her home as usual, but her parents were having one of their parties, and the street was full of trashy cars, and he couldn't park until way down the block. She must have sighed or something, and he turned to her and said with concern, Are you going to be OK?

I think so, Nic had said, but she had tears in her eyes. She could cope with her hard family, with any test thrown her way, with the bitchiness of high school girls and the meatheadedness of high school boys, but when any adult outside her family asked her if she was doing well, she always wept. And then the next second, Richard was leaning over the stick shift and kissing her. She'd been kissed by boys, but never by a man, and from the first time she saw Richard, he stirred up something in her. But also, Nic said to Birdie, girls were different then. She was trying to raise her own daughter so that she'd sock a grown married man who did something like that, but she had been conditioned to want to please men. So, with real lust and hunger to please, she kissed him back. And it felt disgusting, as though she was a bad person—because even after a week, she loved Deanna—but, Nic said now, Oh, Birdie, it was so unbelievably hot.

I bet, Birdie said. You were unbelievably hot then.

They laughed, and Nic said, So that's how it began.

Never before work, but usually after, and sometimes he'd come back to the house during the boy's nap. It was like every part of me had just woken up. All my nerves, all my perceptions, even my sense of taste. A tomato was no longer just a tomato but something much bigger and more beautiful. Every hour of the day and night was nearly unbearable in its depth. And every time I saw Deanna, I felt such tremendous grief, because there was some logical part of me that absolutely knew what I was doing, and that I was harming her.

And then one day, Nic said, she heard the Jaguar come up the drive to the camp during the boy's nap, and her body just responded, it was Pavlovian. But it wasn't Richard who walked in the door, it was Deanna. And she knew then that she had what she deserved coming to her. She was pretending to read on the couch, and Deanna looked at her for a long time from the doorway, wearily, then smiled and said she had wanted to swim so badly, she just took off from her meeting and came home. Then she tossed a bathing suit at Nic, and grabbed one herself, and said, Come on. Nic was pretty sure Deanna was going to lead her out into the middle of the lake to drown her, but she went along because a part of her knew that she deserved it. They swam out far enough but not so far that they wouldn't be able to hear the baby monitor on the dock, and Deanna turned to Nic, and Nic bowed her head, waiting for the harsh and unforgiving words or her hands pressing down on her head.

Then she kissed me, Nic said.

Birdie gasped. I mean, I saw it coming, she said, but damn.

In retrospect, here was this thirty-five-year-old woman whose husband was very obviously sleeping with a child, and here was a way to try to become the master of the whole situation. On the other hand, it was the most beautiful kiss Nic had ever had in her life.

And it awoke that old sleeping beast in you, Birdie said quietly.

It did, Nic said. And then I essentially moved into their guest room. The next two months, with both of them, and the boy to sweeten the whole day, were the very happiest of my life. I think if there is such a thing as heaven, I would be returned to those months in an endless loop. Waiting at night in that bed, trembling when there was a step on the staircase, not knowing who the step belonged to, breathless to see, wanting both of them at the same time, always feeling inordinately confused and yet constantly in a kind of rush of wind. But then the time ran out, and I said goodbye and went off to school. And it was a sudden dislocation from my entire previous life, and the town and my friends, and these people I loved so much were just some kind of dream. I didn't mourn for any of it, because you can't mourn for a dream. But I did find out that they separated later. That's the worst thing I did, driving those good parents away from their little boy.

They thought in silence for a while, and then Birdie slowly said, It's funny. Now I think you wouldn't have been able to see us that summer even if we'd wanted you to. I think I knew all about what was going on, deep down, and that it drove me a little crazy. I know you know that it came from me, the ostracizing. Not Melodie or Sammie. It was me. I was murderous with jealousy, I think.

I know, Nic said.

Of that couple, though. For having you, Birdie said.

I know, Nic said.

What I think I'm trying to say is that I'm sorry for what I did to you. I'm sorry I wrote that letter to your parents in middle school and that your dad. Well, I'm sorry that he hurt you. I'm sorry we couldn't be friends the same way, not even in high school. I'm sorry I killed that beautiful thing in you for so long.

Birdie was crying, but Nic laughed and said, Oh, Bird, it's OK. I *was* a drippy little hanger-on back then. And it's not like we really knew what we were doing to each other in your My Little Pony sleeping bag, anyway. It was all kind of abstract, right? It just felt good. And I definitely agreed back then with everyone, with my god, and your god, and my parents, and with you after you wrote that letter about how perverted I was, that there was and would always be something grotesque in me for wanting to have sex with literally every human being that I saw. Only when I met Richard and Deanna did I understand that it could be good.

Birdie said, Tell me you forgive a dying woman.

Nothing to forgive, but I forgive you, Nic said. I forgave you the moment you sent the letter. You were thirteen. Everyone's an asshole at thirteen. I forgave you in high school when we were finally friends again and you kissed me at Lucky Smith's party and then turned around and hooked up with Lucky. Of course I forgive you now.

There was a knock and Birdie's parents came in, wan in their snow-dusted peacoats. Their one night off from their daughter's deathbed, the true reason for the friends' visit, had visibly been spent in lamentation. Nic hugged them and backed away because with them here, the past was too heavy. Not even a week later, Birdie's mother would call with the news, and Nic would thank her and clutch the phone to her ear long after she hung up, unable to move in the waves of grief and rage that kept crashing over her, until slowly the grief faded away, and only the rage remained. Because she hadn't lied to Birdie, she had in fact forgiven her friend, but the friend she had forgiven was that unspeakably swollen, nearly dead woman in the hospital, and the young Birdie of the silky warm skin so close to her own in the sleeping bag on the green shag carpet of her room, the taste of her in Nic's mouth, the happiness between them. There were only two forgivable Birdies. All the Birdies in between, all those bitches, still had something to answer for.

In the hospital, Nic had stayed on and on until she looked at the clock and saw that it was long past the time when she should have left, and she kissed Birdie on the cheek lingeringly so that she could remember the warmth of her, and flew through the halls of the sick and the suffering, drove wildly to the airport and threw the keys at the rental car valet and bolted to the gate. She rose into the flight, that gorgeous liminal moment that's a respite between lives; and descended again into the grind of the quotidian, collecting her daughter from her estranged husband's house, opening the briefcase full of first-year family law papers, identifying the strange stink as emanating from the garbage, entering the lonely late-night ritual of left-swipes, ignoring the desiccated peas on the kitchen tiles, the bills, the attention-hungry cat that wouldn't stop rubbing herself on Nic's ankle. She sat up at her desk and did not work, but pretended to, and felt the cat circling and circling and pressing herself into Nichole's skin, as though to tell her what words could not, as though these poor mortal bodies of theirs were ever nearly enough to express the terrible depths of love.

What's the Time, Mr. Wolf?

The boy floated with the newts in the dark water of the pond. The points of the pines scorched the sky and a hawk slowly circled the sun. In the shallows, the two dogs were islands of red-gold snout, spine, tail; up in the great house, the women were drinking cold gin from teacups, the men resting naked in shuttered bedrooms under the wind that roared from box fans.

The boy had lain all afternoon in the pond, so long that he was sure the water had entered his brain through his ears and had washed all thought out. He was as dumb as the newts all around him with their fat bellies and splayed limbs. He would lie here suspended beyond the tense hot afternoon and into the dusk with fireflies, he would lie here into the night, into the dawn, into the rest of the summer and the fall with the surface of the pond scummed with red maple leaves and the winter with the cold slowing him until his heart beat once a day and the ice covered him gently as with a thickness of glass. It would be a good life, this life of newt. He would be held up by the dark brown water that lapped at him, that asked nothing at all of him.

Suddenly, out of the sky there fell a fist-size stone that gulped the water close to his head. Another, closer. He rolled upright.

His sister was at the end of the dock and the afternoon sun shone through her pale dress and pricked out her new bony body, shone her hair into a fireball around her head.

Oh, he thought, she has come back to him, his first friend, his Libby as she'd been before she went off to the family school and was earthquaked into this new strange creature of sharp bones and secrets, eating only apples, her eyes made enormous without glasses. The mean new Elizabeth would not throw stones as a joke, but his beloved gawky Libby would, and would help him build forts in the woods and play Uno with flashlights and get him up early so they could run across the lawn still draped in morning fog and sear their feet with dew to giddy pain.

Chip, his sister was yelling. Come up. It's time.

As he neared and lunged as though to grab her feet,

however, he saw the reversion was a trick, Libby was gone for good, angular Elizabeth had long ago eaten her. She stepped away from his grabbing hands. Her mouth was slack, her shoulders loose, and in them he saw that she'd been stealing sips of gin from the women, even though she was only fourteen. She said, in their grandmother's clipped voice, Tell that child to come up and wash himself thoroughly, and with soap, for I will not have pond stink at my Independence Day supper. She smiled, pleased with herself.

How is it? he said. Up there. With Mom.

Shit show, she said, and showed her teeth and began to walk tenderly up the lawn because she was barefoot and there was a shimmering cloth of bees above the clover in the grass.

The dogs pulled themselves wearily from the water, shook rainbows from their fur. His body felt exquisite in the heat after so long in the water, skinless and stripped to nerves. He led the dogs the distance up to the house and left them at the door to the center hall, though he was forbidden to use it when wet. For a moment, his dazzled eyes did not make out Bear standing there, frowning at the newspaper folded in his hands, but then his grandfather cleared his throat and Chip's eyes adjusted and Bear gave him an ostentatious wink and the boy ran up one curve of the stairs and all the way to the children's wing, where his clothes lay like a second, overly starched Chip upon the bed. He could not bear to think of showering off the pond's dark magic and so he put these awful clothes on next to his skin. When he looked down into the hall again, Bear had retreated, and so Chip slid down the banister and leapt off before the finial with its carved pineapple came up fast and clocked him in the groin.

As he passed through the dining room, he saw the caterer with a sheet of light in her hands at the far end, which even as he watched became only a shining membrane of plastic wrap. Her shirt was sweated through and he saw her beige bra biting into the flesh of her back. He should have looked away, he understood this although he was only ten, but he stopped and stared. She turned around and frowned at him, flicking him away with her eyes, and he ran out to the terrace, straight into his dread.

There the women sat in their corners. His grandmother Slim, in her wicker chair spread all around her in a glorious peacock design, his mother, Julia, knotted in her chair with his sister, Elizabeth, perched on the arm beside her, Aunt Diana talking as always, a chunk of amber as large as a baby's fist at her neck catching the sunlight and shining. The story was that Uncle Charley had rescued Diana from a yoga studio when he married her, which explained why she was always saying the kind of thing that she was saying now, Surely the desert is haunted, but in a very special way, you can feel the ghosts just rolling across it like tumbleweeds whenever the sun goes down and the moon rises and the wind dies out, that's when they come out, the ancient ghosts that don't care about anything so paltry as the human, something to do with magnetism, the veins of electricity in the bedrock or something, or the spirits of the stones themselves moving in their infinitely slow way. She laughed.

His mother's eyes had found Chip. She was commanding him to come near. He sat on her lap, though her leg bones were hot and trembling. She held him around the middle and pressed her face into his back. Slim's roses were so lush on the trellises shadowing the veranda that the perfume was a thick invisible wall.

The dogs, having seen Chip come out, tried to climb up to him from the lawn, but Slim grimaced at their wet fur and growled, Down, and they slunk back to the shade of the apple orchard beside the perennial gardens.

Well, isn't it hot, Slim said, interrupting Diana, which wasn't counted as rude because nobody ever listened to Diana, the whole family interrupted her, it was fine. Bear emerged with a frosty shaker in his hand

and bent to refresh the ladies' drinks. I'm getting soused! Diana said. Elizabeth held up her iced tea for a splash, and Bear chuckled and poured a little. Slim looked at Chip's mother to see how she would protest, but their mother's face was buried in Chip's back, and so Elizabeth was allowed her gin, and Slim's disapproval with her daughter, Chip's mother, passed into the continuous unspoken, the family's syntax of silence.

Now the caterer came out with an apron to cover her sweated-through shirt, and said, I'm finished, ma'am.

Thank you, Jolene, Slim said. She closed her eyes and tilted her face to a strip of sun; she did not believe in tipping.

And when the woman twisted her red hands in her apron, and did not move, and then as the seconds ticked on and the woman folded her mouth into a determined slit, Slim said, Oh, are you still here? Well. Surely your family misses you. Have a lovely Independence Day.

When the caterer left, Bear followed her out, because one of his family jobs was to stealthily fix what Slim in her imperiousness broke; he would tip well.

When Bear returned to the veranda, Uncle Charley was behind him, and Chip had to stifle a laugh, because they were both sunburned from the morning's golf, both in pink shirts, his uncle was just a smaller, plumper, blonder version of his grandfather. But, then again, so was Chip, the youngest of these three Charleses. He wondered if each younger Charles always came out a little worse than the one before, going back all the way to the very first Charles, who had come to Boston from England and made the family very very rich oh ages ago. He hoped not. Then he made a fervent wish inside himself that Uncle Charley and Aunt Diana would have the baby they were working so hard to make, and that it would be a boy and that they would name him Charles, and he would become the true Charles of the generation, so that Chip could be released from this string of diminishment, could become something separate from the rest. By the sadness in Aunt Diana's face, the baby wouldn't be coming soon.

Uncle Charley took the bourbon his father poured him, and took a gulp and coughed and said, Are we still waiting for Flippy?

Everyone knew: Drinks were at five, and supper was at six, for eating too late in the day undermined the proper workings of the tripes, as Slim always said.

Why would he come? Elizabeth said. I'm sure he's super pissed.

Chip's mother twitched under him, and he felt her face move against his back, perhaps into a smile. Slim glinted dangerously at her granddaughter and swallowed the girl's impertinence up with a laugh.

And so they waited, and into the waiting Diana spoke of high colonics and the concept of nirvana and Slim spoke approvingly of Nancy Reagan's shoes and hair, and Bear genially told stories of his family's eccentrics, the granduncle who married a Paris cancan dancer, the great-grandmother who ran away on her wedding day and was discovered in a house of disrepute in New Orleans, but who was returned to her life and had six children and became an exemplary philanthropist, putting her name on a concert hall in Boston. From the stereo system, the music poured low, Rachmaninoff, the afternoon settled, the shadows stretched and darkened on the lawn. In the village down the hill early fireworks burst even though it was still too light to see them. The dogs came around to the kitchen door, and the housekeeper brought them in and fed them, then released them back into the evening, then brought the family little bowls of hot nuts on a tray. And still Flip did not come.

At last, at seven, Slim said, Well, my youngest has always been his own man. To supper we go. And they all followed her into the dining room, Diana wobbly in her heels from the gin.

There were tiny flags on the buffet, a whole poached salmon under cucumber scales, a bowl of fresh mayonnaise, a salad wilted from the wait, hard rolls, pats of butter molded into stars on mostly melted ice. The housekeeper had folded the red-and-white-striped napkins into patriotic swans. The family filled their plates in silence and sat at the overlong table. Chip's mother took nothing, and put her children on either side of her. Chip could feel her body trembling through the legs of her chair, over the floorboard, and up his own chair's legs, into his body.

When everyone had taken a seat, Bear stood up and smiled genially at the head of the table and lifted his glass and cleared his throat, and here was the awful moment coming, Chip closed his eyes and took his mother's damp tight fist in his hand, and this was when they all heard an engine roaring, the sound of wheels spinning too fast through gravel and music thudding inside a car, Flip's car, at last; Uncle Flip had finally come.

How very like my boy, Slim said icily. To arrive only when we'd given up all hope for him.

They listened as the engine shut off, the car doors shut, the footsteps nearly running over the gravel, the great hall door opened and slammed, shaking the chandelier above the dining table into a wild tinkling. And here was Flip in the doorway, shouting, Hallooo, hallooooo. He was sweaty, his hair in stiff spikes and his eyes protuberant. Chip heard his sister hiss and say under her breath, Jesus, coke much?

Behind him, hesitantly, there appeared a woman. She was very tall, at least Bear's height, and her enormous cascade of black curls fell to her abdomen. She was wearing a star-spangled miniskirt and a sequined red top, her face heavy with makeup, red lipstick, blue eyeshadow, but she was not at all pretty, with the bridge of her nose like a knot between her close-set eyes and a huge jaw that reminded Chip of a bulldog's. She was older than Flip, closer to Chip's mother's age.

Hi, she said softly, and held up a six-pack of beer.

How lovely, Philip, you brought someone, Slim said, and did not stand or reach out for the beer.

Family, I'd like to present my lovely friend I just met down at the pizza joint in the village, what's your name again?

Pearl Spang, the woman said, and put the beer down on the buffet. I thought you said this was going to be a cookout, Philip.

Pearl Spang, what a wonderful name! Flip said.

You are welcome here, Pearl, Uncle Charley said in his new unctuous voice.

And how very festive you look, Slim said, and the corner of her mouth twitched.

Please, Pearl, eat eat eat, Flip said, gesturing at the buffet, and Pearl obediently turned to fill a plate. Flip pulled a chair out, spun it around so it faced backward, and straddled it. He looked at Chip's mother, and she looked back, and between the brother and sister there ran such a dark electricity that Chip for the first time during this long, strange day felt scared.

Don't let me interrupt you, Bear, Flip said. Looks like you were about to give a big old speech there.

Pearl Spang carried her full plate to the empty chair next to Chip and sat, and her perfume, musky and warm, went up his nostrils, he could taste it, and he closed his eyes to smell it deeper. A curious thing happened in his body, something like a wave crashed through it. Beside his own untouched plate, for it was only good manners to refrain from eating until all the speeches had been spoken, he saw the bright nails and the broad hands rapidly spearing fish, lifting the bites, bringing the clean tines back down to the plate; he could hear Pearl chewing and feel her warmth emanating toward him, but he could not look at her face.

Bear hefted himself to his feet again, and raised his glass. I was about to say before you arrived, Flippy, how grateful I am to be gathered here today, on the birthday of our great nation, at our old estate, with my beloved family. And new friends, Bear said, winking at Pearl.

Bear said how glad he was that the family showed its solidarity by coming. It could not have been easy to wake up to the news, and Bear was angry, really quite quite quite angry that the *Globe* had published it a week before he had put the final plans in place, but you can't trust a journalist farther than you can throw one, ha ha, and quite obviously Bear and Slim were committed to equality between all three of their children, they would certainly balance the scales and make sure Philip and Julia were given equal portions of the family fortune in the will to make up for the imbalance, and none of this should be seen as a referendum on who is the favored child or who is loved more, or any such nonsense as that. Of course not. Oh, no, this was simply business. Bear and Slim had had many long years of discussions, a great deal of heartache, you better believe it, but in the end they felt it was right that Charles become CEO of the bank, which, of course, bears his name.

To all of my brilliant children, Bear intoned, raising a glass, but today is Charles's day, so to Charles today. Only Slim and Diana raised theirs, smiling. Uncle Charley was flushed, his eyes gleaming with pleasure.

Pearl's plate was already half-empty; on the other side, his mother's breathing had become ragged. Her nails pressed into Chip's hand and burned but he didn't withdraw.

Truly, Uncle Flip said in his unnaturally high and fast voice, what an unbelievably Waspy thing to do, how passive-aggressive can you get, telling two out of three children they've been disinherited in the business pages of *The Boston Globe*.

Oh, don't be so dramatic, Flip, Slim said. Nobody is disinherited.

Ah, dramatic, Flip said, what a perfect word, it's true there's little more dramatic than waking up to find that your older brother who knows nothing at all about banks has been given everything. Charley, who, and forgive me, I don't mean to be rude, but it's the truth, is by far the least qualified of the three of us. A sports agent. You put a motherfucking sports agent in charge of a three-hundred-year-old bank.

The skill set is transferable, Charley said in a tight voice.

While I, Flip said, speaking over his brother, am the only one with an MBA and have been at the bank for five years and know it like the back of my hand. But fuck me, when poor Julia has been at the bank for twenty years, Julia, who came up through the mail room as a high schooler, which, I'll remind you, Bear never made Charley and me do, of course, when Julia, who worked her way to VP on her own merit, sacrificing her own sweat and tears and missing her kids' childhoods and losing even her marriage to the bank, Julia, who is the oldest and the smartest and the one who deserves it the most, gets nothing. Nothing for Julia! Zilch! Zero! Nothing but the morning paper telling her that her intelligence and work mean literally nothing to this family because she had the misfortune of being born with a cunt. And because Charley, forgive me, but the family fucking idiot, is the one with the name.

Ad hominem. Extremely unfair, Charley said.

Let's all take a few cleansing breaths, Aunt Diana whispered.

It is exactly this behavior that disqualified you, Philip, Slim said. You are simply too flamboyant, it's a matter of our clients' comfort, that they can see themselves in the captain of the ship. You and Julia are frankly impossible. Among the three of you, only Charley could possibly make them feel secure.

Just imagine what our clients' wives would think if their husbands went off to play golf with Julia every weekend. And you don't even play golf, Flippy, Bear said.

Besides, Slim said. Your . . . Well, your tastes, Philip. We've never said anything. Live and let live, this is our motto. But imagine the scandal if it got out.

Flip blinked slowly. Slim's frown faded and a softness came into her face as she looked at him, her youngest child, the one who looked the most like her. At last Flip said, You know? You've known?

Oh, please, Slim said, I am your mother. Since you were born.

I mean, you had a life-size poster of Paul Newman on your closet door when you were twelve, Uncle Charley said, chuckling.

My goodness, Diana said into the new and ringing silence. If it matters at all to you, Flip, I never even suspected.

Beside Chip, Pearl Spang bent over, and the ends of her long black curly hair brushed Chip's thigh, and she removed her high heels with both hands, and stood, barefoot, then backed away from the table, snagging the six-pack of beer as she passed the buffet, and stepped through the doors to the veranda and there was swallowed up by the twilight.

I think I'm going crazy, Uncle Flip said at last, tugging at the shocked ends of his hair. This is insane. I'm going insane.

This whole family is fucking crazy, Elizabeth said, slurring her words.

Language, Elizabeth, Uncle Charley said; and with this, Elizabeth took the hard roll from her plate, and threw it at him so quickly that it bounced off his sunburned forehead, though the pat of butter in the shape of a star stuck on his skin and slowly began to slide down.

Then, into the shocked silence, Elizabeth said, We're going, Mama, and pulled their mother up out of her chair, then out the door into the hall, and Chip ran after, grabbing their mother's pocketbook from the closet, and then they, too, had passed through the vast doors into the breathing heat of evening, the navy sky with the hanging moon, the frog song rising from the pond, the distant crackle of fireworks down the mountain. Elizabeth put their mother into the passenger seat, and though she was only fourteen, and rather drunk, she started the car and drove it, bucking and squealing, around the gravel circle, down the drive, and out onto the dirt road, where the eyes of night creatures peered greenly out of the thickening dark.

Elizabeth stopped the car in the pull-off before the road that ran down the mountain into the village, leaned her head against the steering wheel, and sobbed dryly.

I hate them, she said at last.

I know, honey, their mother said. Me, too.

Chip looked at his mother, who seemed strong now, and calm. Her chin was jutted and dangerous. She looked a great deal like Slim.

Eventually, his mother and sister switched seats, and their mother put the car in gear again, and they glided out into the road.

When they were moving, something horrifying rose up from very deep in Chip's body, something he tried to push down again, and he couldn't help himself; he put his hands over his mouth, but the laughter was stronger than he was, it came out of him choking and awful.

Elizabeth turned and frowned at him, then the old Libby smile came over her face. Uncle Charley, she said. The butter slipping down. And then she, too, started to laugh.

Now even their mother was laughing. I'm starving, she said at last when she calmed. We'll stop and get a slice of pizza in town. But this made the kids laugh even harder.

Pizza. Pearl Spang, Elizabeth gasped. That fucking six-pack.

And this way down they went on the road twisting through the forest, and a firework burst up from the lake every so often and lit the tops of the trees in pink and orange and green and gold. Chip wiped his face on his sleeve. Out in the thickness of the woods, on the hiking trail that connected Maine to Georgia, which ran beside the road here, he caught a glimpse of a shadow moving quickly, a flare of red sequins in the headlights, but then the car moved on and all was dark and hidden in the woods again.

CHIP'S MOTHER NEVER RETURNED to the bank; with lethal silence, she started up her own firm, taking a dozen of the bank's more progressive clients with her. She put everything she had into it and had to sell the lovely white house on Beacon Hill, and Chip and she moved into a condominium with beige carpets in the North End. Uncle Flip went west to Hollywood to be a producer, Elizabeth back to boarding school, which Slim and Bear still paid for, although neither Elizabeth nor Chip's mother was speaking to them. Only Chip fielded the phone calls, awkward, monosyllabic, for fear his mother would overhear and be hurt. But she was hardly ever around, and, on weekdays, Chip walked to school, walked back, did his homework with the television on, reheated what the house cleaner left for his supper, put himself to bed. On weekend mornings, he waited on the hall floor outside his mother's room until she came out in her mint-green kimono, mascara smeared under her eyes.

It was with a sense of relief all around that Chip went off to the family boarding school as a freshman. Elizabeth was a senior, her bony face gentling whenever she saw her brother. Her smile blazed up into his solitude and warmed him.

Time sped up, blurred. Bluestone chapel in the mornings, blue blazer, blue ink in the exam books, lonely blue mornings full of fog. His mother's letters arrived on Tuesdays, the phone calls with Slim and Bear were scheduled on Sunday nights on the hall phone for exactly four minutes, mostly taken up with news of intramural lacrosse though Chip wasn't very good, being plump and slow and uncoordinated, and in return Slim and Bear told him what animals they had seen on their hikes in the desert where they had moved: coyotes, roadrunners, javelinas. The summer was split between the family estate with the pond the forest the hikes up the mountains, cocktail hour, a figure in the far fields, walking swiftly, a dog leaping at its feet, the housekeeper's hot nuts, and the woozy humid days in Boston, the empty condominium. Then one week just before school in August at their father's in the Caymans. Their father had become, as Elizabeth said, a tax pirate. He looked like one, all ruddy with sun and drink, seemingly unable to place his children when they came into the room. Boarding school again, dimmer now without Elizabeth in it to shoot him a smile, she being in freshman year at the college the family had gone to for centuries, and the one good moment of his week was opening his mailbox to find her letter in it, thick and funny and slightly smelling of apples. College was good for her, she loved it, she got a nose ring, she partied in the city, she now had a girlfriend, yes she was a lesbian. Uncle Flip has just been so supportive, she wrote, but don't tell Mama, yet; Elizabeth wanted to come out to her in person. Just as the snow melted, she wrote for him to spend the summer with her and her friends on Martha's Vineyard, they're all getting restaurant jobs, and he, thinking of the empty condo, the family estate with Slim and Bear slowly getting potted from five p.m. on, said hell yes and came out to the island and slept on a blow-up pool float for two months. Boats in the bay and jugs of cold wine in the fridge, and girl panties in the bathroom drying on the line, and noises from the bedrooms late at night that made him burn with hunger and embarrassment. Chip's forearms chiseled from scooping ice cream out of rock-hard containers all summer. The tacit understanding was that Chip and Elizabeth did not have to visit their father in the Caymans this year, and they were a little hurt when he didn't press the issue. Back to junior year with sun streaks in his hair, the acne gone from the sea salt and tan, and, surprise! Chip was suddenly sort of popular. All you have to do is say nothing and laugh at everything and you get a reputation for being jolly. House parties, ski trips, weekends at second houses in Nantucket, third houses in the Berkshires, penthouses in

Manhattan, nightclubs everywhere, fake IDs, Molly and pot and vodka in his orange juice in the back of history class. One morning, a blurry memory of girl legs, a bared breast, a smeared mouth, weeping, just some townie whose face he couldn't remember, and his friends a little awkward when Chip came into the room but soon class solidarity flowed around him again like water. He was hungover for his SATs, they were so awful that Bear talked to him in a sad voice and Slim hired him a daily tutor and promised a BMW for hitting 1350, a Mercedes for more than 1400. On his third try, he got a 1320, and they relented and gave him a car; it was only a Volvo, but it was new. Another summer on the Vineyard. He was a barback at his sister's restaurant, there were parties every night after closing, cigarettes in the alleyway, Bloody Marias for hair of the dog when the sunrise sent swords into his eyes. Senior year, parties and sleeping during calculus, and on the phone one Sunday, Bear cleared his throat and said, I'm so sorry your grades are not what we would expect for you to follow your sister, well, to follow the whole family, to the college, and you may want to look at less challenging schools, Chippy. But Slim said sharply on the other line, Charles, are you utterly insane? He's a legacy a hundred times over and there is nothing that the right donation cannot do. And, as usual, Slim was correct. He was accepted with his mediocre SATs and grades, even though the class valedictorian, a girl who was captain of three sports and had perfect SATs, was not, and when she was told she would not be let in off the wait list, she began to ugly-cry in chapel and had to be led out by her friends and comforted under the apple trees just then blowing their white petals everywhere. Prom, a blurry boob unearthed from blue chiffon, Martha's Vineyard. His sister staggering home, and against the rising sun she seemed transparent, she had so little flesh upon her bones. The Caymans, their father deflated, leathery, dating a girl younger than Elizabeth. Chip had forgotten how utterly spiky Elizabeth could be. Their father's girl vanished and was not seen again during their stay.

COLLEGE WAS ALL NEW until the second week. Chip moved himself shyly through the days, and then it was simply prep school all over again in a different place. Same old faces, same old parties, same beer pong and midnight pizza, ecstasy and blow and Adderall and pot, someone's dad's box at the Celtics, someone's house on the Cape. He saw Elizabeth every Sunday for brunch until he slept through two in a row and she took to barging into his dorm with bagels and coffee to make sure he was alive, not that his sister would ever eat a bagel. She had become so skinny that she worried him; he was afraid the wind off the Charles would snap her like a twig. Spring break at their father's in the Caymans because he was getting married suddenly, small wedding, but Elizabeth was not there in the sun and heat with Chip, and their mother was not there, either, although things had grown cordial between his parents, and it was only when Chip flew back to freezing Boston that he found out Elizabeth had collapsed in an elevator, was in a hospital, was being force-fed and was too embarrassed to see him, though Slim and Bear came to visit her every day, and through these visits, their mother began speaking to her parents for the first time since they'd made Charley head of the bank. Elizabeth did her schoolwork in the hospital, returned to her courses with a vengeance, graduated summa, began to work at their mother's firm. Their mother with a sleek angular new haircut and eyes made up smokily; oh, how his women are so beautiful, Chip thought, as his mother and Elizabeth came laughing together into the restaurant for their weekly Thursday dinner. He saw his mother as young enough to marry again, and felt a little strange about the idea. Your sister is a superstar, their mother said over appetizers. A natural. A genius. She raised her glass of champagne, and Chip and Elizabeth raised and downed their own.

His grades weren't great but were good enough. Martha's Vineyard in the summers, but there was better pay working in construction there for his buddy's uncle than as a barback, and he learned to demolish, tile, build, and roof. He graduated, no honors, but with an extensive group of friendly acquaintances. His mother did not offer him a job and he did not think he should have to ask. Uncle Charley eventually did. Chip was summoned to lunch on his first day, and sat across from his uncle, both with their napkins tucked into their collars, and his uncle looked at him kindly over his glasses as they ate lukewarm clam chowder. At least I got one of you kids over here. Your sister is a tough one, he said. Refuses, though we'd give a two hundred percent raise. And it's looking less and less likely Diana and I will be having kids of our own, you know, she's getting past the point where it makes any sense to keep on and the doctors haven't helped in years. Years and years. Heartbreak. In any event, looks like you're what we've got. So work hard, Chippy. Keep your head down. You'll be the pride of the family yet, won't you? You'll make us all proud, my boy.

Sure, Chip said, feeling warm. Of course he would

make his family proud, he had no choice, after all. Everything had been decided for him long before he was born.

Chip liked his job fine. He liked his coworkers, they were low-key buddies, they drank together every night, went to each other's weddings, and when some left the bank to do other things, they fell easily and without too much fuss out of one another's lives. Some of the guys he started with were promoted, even though Chip was not, but it was certainly, he was sure, because Uncle Charley and Bear didn't want to make the very public mistake of nepotism. He bought a condo he barely lived in, saw women who were just a tad not right enough to introduce to his sister and his mother: too plain, state-school graduate, only an admin assistant. They never lasted very long and were gone in a month or so. There were three years of this, four years. Once there was a bad story, a girl invited home when they were both too drunk to see straight, something happened in the bedroom that Chip honestly didn't remember, waking to pain, then the police, charges brought, only to be dropped when Slim stepped in, and Chip was let off, and it all passed into the perpetual unspoken. The family pressed closer around Chip, it seemed, wary and concerned.

Then his mother married abruptly, a bald man aptly

named Rich who cycled hundreds of miles a week and was as slender and elegant as a crane. Elizabeth and Chip stood outside the courthouse and kissed their mother's cheeks, on which were mixed the warm spring rain and her tears, and Elizabeth rested her head on Chip's shoulder as they watched the taxi whisk their mother and her new husband away through the wet gray streets. I'm happy, their mother had whispered to them over her corner-kiosk lilies. Oh, kids, I'm so happy, and I had given up on happiness long ago. I didn't think it was for me. Then she was gone and it was her happiness that lingered on the street with them, that made them feel shy and embarrassed.

Celebratory drink? Chip said. He saw Elizabeth so little these days. She had taken up marathon running and worked all the time, even the weekends. He thought hopefully of a corner booth, bourbon, Elizabeth's devil taking over and her scalding mimicry of their family, Slim's clipped scorn and Bear's slow geniality and Diana's airy sadness and Flip's manic and scattered brilliance. But his sister sighed and rubbed her face. Oh, Chippy, I don't drink anymore. It just exacerbated everything.

Chip laughed, because this was absurd, and then he saw she was serious.

But you're not an alcoholic, he said. You're totally normal.

She shivered and pulled her scarf closer to her neck, and said, Yeah, well, in a family where alcoholism is the norm, normal isn't good. She kissed him, and looked at him as though she was about to say more, and so he turned and hurried away, shouting over his shoulder to have her assistant call him to schedule lunch sometime this week. There was a time when he would have let her boss him, would have allowed her to tell him that maybe he should stop drinking, he had a problem, he'd missed two business lunches in the past month because he'd had Bloody Marys for breakfast and wound up sleeping at his desk. One of the funny family stories was that when he was still crawling, she'd begged for a collar and a leash and put it on him, and for a long time he thought he was a puppy, and sat when she told him to sit, rolled over at her command. Now he was a grown man, twenty-five, no puppy; he had learned the art of slipperiness when things became too heavy for him to hold.

Six months after their mother's wedding to Rich, Chip's desk phone rang, and his uncle asked him to come up to his office. Chip tried to play it cool, but this was certainly his promotion, at long last he could pay off his credit card debts, rent a place on the Vineyard for a few weeks next summer, and pay back the friends who had spotted him all these years. He composed his face in the shining brass of the elevator doors, pressed his fair thinning curls down, brushed the bagel seeds off his suit jacket, and frowned to make his soft face look older than it was.

When he came into his uncle's office, Charley was leaning back in his chair and Bear was standing at the window. His grandfather turned and silently opened his arms for a hug, and Chip felt like a child again, engulfed by Bear's warmth and expensive pine-and-leather cologne. His grandfather's Arizona tan was so deep that his crow's-feet were white rays around his eyes.

Chippy! Uncle Charley said. Sit, sit. Chip sat, blood thudding in his ears. Bear returned to the window to face Boston, the shard of slate that was the harbor; it felt strange to Chip that his grandfather was turning his back on him.

Before we begin, you need to know that we have a plan, don't worry, you're family. You will always, always be taken care of, Uncle Charley said, tenting his hands over his belly. The October sun in its sideways tilt through the window shone through his sparse hair. You're like the son I never had. All this to say that Bear and I gave you four years, kid, but we just don't think you're cut out for banking. Your numbers are just not there. I'm sorry.

Funny business this, Bear said. You've got to act like a trained dog, but be a wolf inside. Turns out you're no wolf, buddy.

Which is not necessarily a bad thing, Charley said. You'll probably have a better life, to be honest. We just have to find a position in the company where you're a better match. We were thinking in the real estate division. It's all people skills, which you're good at, and the lawyers are the ones doing the tricky stuff under the surface.

Chip's mind, which had slowed in surprise, finally caught up. He clutched his hands and said, You're firing me?

Oh no. No no no, Uncle Charley said with a pained smile. Just moving you along to where your gifts can shine.

You're firing me, Chip said. Plus you're calling me stupid.

No, you're not stupid, Bear said with his chuckle. Just perhaps not as motivated as you might be in the position where we first put you.

Chip could feel the tears rising behind his eyes. To save himself, he stood abruptly and walked fast to the elevator, and the doors slid open even as his uncle stood and called after him and a rare anger passed over Bear's face. Then the doors closed, and Chip descended.

He left everything in his cubicle, the overcoat and scarf and attaché case, all of which were expensive gifts from Slim, and breathed the cold air on the sidewalk for a time. The sunlight off the grass of the Common was far too bright in his eyes. It felt like an assault. People all around were moving too fast, and there should have been noise, car noise, plane noise, noise of music and voices, but there was nothing, everything was dulled and silent.

He walked as fast as he could, stopping to buy two handles of bourbon, and, once home, stripped to his underwear, pulled down the shades, and fell into obliteration.

His sister gave him three days. On the third, she let herself in with her key. She gagged, then threw open all the windows and stood angrily in her tight pantsuit, fists on hips, surveying the chicken-wing bones, the ice cream pints abandoned and leaking, the strewn pizza, the dribbling bottles. You're a fucking pig, Chippy, she said.

Oink, he said.

She pulled him upright, pushed him into the bathroom, turned on the hot shower, shoved him into it even though he was still in his underwear. He stood under the hot water, periodically lapping at it, until it went cold, and when he came into his bedroom, his sister had packed a suitcase and was sweeping everything on his coffee table into a trash bag with a broom. Grab a coat, she said. Car's downstairs. The driver's waiting.

But, he said, I have things to attend. He was sought after. There was a gallery opening, there was a gala for the art museum, he was hosting a table.

They'll survive without you, Elizabeth said dryly.

As the car moved off, he fell asleep immediately, and when he woke, Elizabeth was poring over files on the seat beside him. In the window, fields spun by under threatening low clouds. The prodigal son's awake, she said. I'm drying you out. The big house is closed but Slim and Bear are going to let you use the caretaker's cottage until you pull your shit together.

But they fired me, he said.

Jesus, Chippy, she said. You would be happier doing literally anything else. That's the worst part. Not that they fired you, that they let you take the job at all. You were never meant for this life.

He turned his face toward the window so that she wouldn't see his expression and when he got control over himself again, he said, So you think I'm an idiot, too.

She hesitated for so long that he despaired, oh, he hated himself so much, and when she at last spoke she said, No. You're not an idiot, but I think you were born lucky. And sometimes luck is a bad thing because you never had to find out what it was you were good at or loved to do. And now you're going to have a lot of time alone to ask yourself these questions. And this is a different kind of luck, which you can't see right now, but you will someday.

It was dusk when they arrived, and twenty degrees colder than it had been in Boston. The great house was sleeping, windows shut-eyed. They fetched the key from the mudroom and, through the glass of the French doors, saw the furniture tucked into its white sheets, the chandelier suspended ghostly above, the ancestors watching dour and patient from the shadows along the walls.

Out over the grass to the caretaker's cottage tucked against the woods. It hadn't been inhabited for twenty years, since Slim began hiring a housekeeper and a landscaping crew from the village for the summer and a contractor to check on the house once or twice a week in the winter, but, as with everything in Slim's empire, it was scrupulously neat. The walls were knotty pine, the floors yellow linoleum, a wood-burning stove took up most of the room in the living space, green cakes of mouse poison sat in every cabinet and corner. There was a metal bed with a mattress still in its great plastic cover. Elizabeth bounced on it and the bedsprings screamed. I had the mattress delivered this afternoon, she said. She flicked the light switches and ran the water and nodded with satisfaction to see that someone had come by to turn it all on.

He watched his sister unpack the groceries she had thought to pick up before coming to get him, mostly vegetables, rice, canned tuna and meat, then she opened a duffel and took from it a towel and sheets she'd packed in his condo. His sister was a wonder, he thought, as he made the fire, and he felt resentful toward her for her thoughtfulness, her organization.

They made a salad together but neither ate much. I see you've got me in low-rent fat camp, he said, slapping his belly so it jiggled. She didn't laugh. Low-rent rehab, more like it, she countered. Slim said you can go ahead and take whatever you need from the great house. The keys to the Jeep are on the hook in the mudroom, if you want to go for groceries or whatever. Then the thing in her that was brittle and angry softened, and tears filled her eyes, and she squeezed his hand. I'm leaving tonight, she said. I have a breakfast meeting. Slim and Bear's phone service is off but there's a phone down in the village at the general store. You be sure to call me at six every Friday at work, yes? So I know you're alive.

How long will I be in exile? he said, thinking of Slim and Bear's liquor cabinet, though it seemed countries away in that old house full of family ghosts.

That's up to you, Elizabeth said, and slapped him lightly on the cheek, then kissed him. We're planning a family Thanksgiving here, maybe you'll be good by then.

When Elizabeth's car had pulled away and silence poured in to fill where the noise and the light had been, he locked the door against the night. He looked in all the closets and pulled out an old green military blanket that had been nibbled at the corners by mice. There were also two neatly folded sets of overalls, clean but paint-spattered, which, though they had sat unused for two decades, still smelled like detergent and pipe tobacco and another man's body. He pulled his new mattress near the woodstove, and lay under the blanket, listening to the forest noises, which had become so loud he doubted he would be able to sleep at all.

When he woke, the fire was out. In the windows a gray dawn moved over the lawn in curls of fog. His head ached, and he felt a terrible darkness in him when he understood that it was aching because it had been a very long time since he had met the dawn sober. He drank three jars of water, pissed out the door, then lay back down on the mattress and slept until midday.

He felt cleaner when he awoke. He put on one of the pairs of overalls he'd found, and his sneakers, and went for a walk where there used to be a trail through the wood. He got lost and, hours later, ended up down at the beaver pond, the wind a frigid whip snapping off the water. His hands shook and he told himself it was from cold. When he climbed back up to the cottage, he found an axe in the shed, and a whetstone, and tried to sharpen the head, then spent a while teaching himself how to chop wood.

Back out into the twilight, sore, with the flashlight, to try to find the far pond, the much larger one where distant generations of his family had learned to sail as children in small wooden boats. During his childhood months at the estate, when he and Elizabeth had roasted marshmallows out there on summer nights, the fireflies flickering doubled against the water and the moon leering down enormous, Bear had come out to visit them and tell stories of the family. Their favorite was the one about Bear's uncle, a rakish handsome boy who had taken a village girl out on a rowboat one night, but the girl ended up mysteriously drowned. The uncle had died young. Heartbroken, they all said, his life ruined by the inquest and unfair rumors of murder. The lovers haunt the pond even now, Bear said solemnly, then stood with the lantern and left the children to put out the fire and camp in the boathouse alone. Later, when Elizabeth was sleeping in her hammock in the boathouse, Chip stayed awake, blinking up at the rafters, hearing a low sighing all the way around the building and thinking of the drowned girl with weeds in her hair, her flesh purple and swollen with water. He turned the flashlight on in pulses to make sure his sister was still in her hammock beside him, and could fall asleep only with her face uplit.

It was almost night when Chip found this larger pond, windless and still under the half-moon, though the mountain in the distance was aflame with last light. The boathouse seemed sturdy, despite its broken windows. Inside, he found evidence of teenage parties, beer cans heaped in a corner, graffiti everywhere, a spent condom like a crushed grub on the floor. But the boats were still neatly stacked, the sails furled and hanging from the rafters to keep the mice out, even the oars for the most part whole on their racks.

He went out to the end of the splintered dock and looked back at the Victorian building, its filigreed woodwork shedding paint, and he understood as he looked that restoring it would be his first project. He had learned those summers in college, had found he had a knack for this kind of work. He would earn his keep. On the way back through the woods, he dreamed of chipping off the paint by hand, reglazing the windows. He went to bed so early that he felt silly, and was at the hardware store in the village as soon as it opened, putting the caulk and glass, the scrapers and primers and paint and brushes, a new door lock, on Slim and Bear's account.

Then he worked. He had never in his life used his body so constantly. He was sunburned, callused by the end of the first week, so sore that moving out of his bed in the morning brought tears to his eyes. He had dragged an old horsehair sofa out of the barn where all the family furniture was left when it lost a leg or was replaced by the whims of the new generation, and risked the great house at midday to fill his arms with books from the library, and spent the evenings after his meal near the woodstove, reading. The last great reader of the family had been Bear's grandmother, and there were thousands of crumbly novels from the turn of the twentieth century. They, like the physical work of the boathouse, felt impossible at first and then, through steadiness and Chip's having nothing else to do, they became easier, then natural to him.

After this first week, Chip remembered the rifles Bear had bought when, for a time in the eighties, he thought he would be a big-game hunter, before he understood that he had no relish for killing. He found them on the walls in Bear's study, the shells in a desk drawer, and one afternoon, when his hands were too blistered and painful to go back to work after lunch, he lined a fence with a row of cans and practiced shooting. This, too, became a part of his silent days, the crack of the rifle before dinner, the cans pinging off into the weeds, the slow mastery.

WHEN HE CALLED his sister the second Friday of his exile, he spoke about how the boathouse was coming along, but neglected to mention the guns, knowing she would not approve. He told her he had deep-cleaned the interior, fixed the windows, it could be a little chapel when the light hit it, and was now scraping the loose ancient paint from the exterior. He heard the smile in her voice when she said, That's great, Chippy. It's so great that you have a project. It took all the strength he had to not smash the telephone down, she was so patronizing, she was treating him like a child. He breathed for a while, his eyes shut against the ugly light of the general store. Yes, he said at last. Isn't it cute, my little project, and she didn't hear the acid in his voice, or perhaps she didn't suspect that he had any acid in him, as he never had shown any before; he had been a lonely child, and then the alcohol must have dulled it out of him.

One afternoon in the third week of his solitude, he was on a ladder scraping the trim near the boathouse's peak when he saw movement in the corner of his eye, and turned his head in time to see a small dog at the far end leaping into the pond after a stick. The dog swam back to shore and shook itself, and the tinkle of its collar bounced across the surface of the water and toward Chip. He descended the ladder and wiped his hands on a rag. He had seen so few people these past few weeks, only the cashier at the general store in the village and the clerk at the gas station, and they had traded only a handful of words. His heart was pounding.

He went along the path to meet the trespasser, and the dog was there first. It was a collie, but a tiny one, a silly little creature that smiled and wagged and shoved its sharp nose into his crotch. Chip was on his knee petting the dog when its owner came around the bend and stopped in the path. Hey, she said warily.

Hey, he said, looking upward at her, and then something in his chest gave a squeeze because he knew this face, the lush lips and Roman nose, the long black curls now daubed at the temples with gray. She had small shoulders, great round hips and thighs, and was looking at him curiously, frowning. He had the vertiginous feeling that she was the authority here, she belonged; that, although this was his family land, he was the interloper.

And he searched wildly in his mind, until there returned to him a short skirt, red sequins, flags on fingernails, a musty perfume that had stirred him in Boston every time a woman walked by and trailed it behind her. Yes. What was her name? Pearl Spang. He remembered now because it was what Elizabeth always called a waitress who was too chummy, a drunk girl peeing on the street, Republican women, vulgar people in general. She had become a family story, had passed into a sobriquet. Pearl Spang.

The woman gave a grunt and clicked her tongue and the dog slunk back to her. Boathouse coming along good, she said.

He stood, and this did not help his sense of being wrong-footed, because Pearl Spang was a head taller than he. Thank you, he said.

I been admiring your work when we take walks up here. My dog and me.

Oh, he said. The moment to say that this was private property and she should not be here at all vanished over the horizon.

We hike up on the back of the mountain, on the

class-six roads, she said. Through the town forest, I live near it. Anyways. After all these years, it's strange to have someone up at this place at this time of year. Usually summer folk, those rich old people who own the place, sometimes they come up Thanksgiving, Christmas. All a sudden, they had someone living here, a surprise. We were all pretty curious about what's going on with you and everything. They hire you? You're here as a caretaker? That's my theory. They're getting old and need someone to keep a steady eye on the place.

Yep, he said, and he flushed with the lie, and to cover it, he said, You want to take a look inside the boathouse?

Sure, she said, and he led the way around the side of the pond, and opened the door for her. She stepped in, whistling. So pretty, she said. Like a church or something. All that wavy light off the pond. I only knew it from when we snuck in to party as kids and it was kind of freaky and shadowy. Gross old mattress that saw lots of cherries popped on it. Every so often, they toss it out, clean the place up, and the kids'd wait until the old people took off in the fall to come back up and make it theirs again. You fix up the loft? she said, and didn't wait for him, but went up the stairs and said from above, Man, that's pretty.

I were you? she said, coming back down. I'd put

hammocks back up there. Nice place to sleep in the summer. They used to do that back in the olden days. How long you here for?

As long as I can stand it, he said, and she laughed.

Well, she said. There's no need for you to be a hermit. We're a little standoffish, it's true, that old Yankee wariness you hear about, but you'll find us nice enough when you get to know us. Come down to the Italian restaurant in town, it's my place, I'll buy you a beer. My name's Pearl.

I'm Chip, he said, and she smiled, her face dimpled and sunny and suddenly quite lovely. There was a shiver in him to know now, definitively, that she, who had taken up so much of his imagination since that awful Independence Day more than fifteen years ago, hadn't recognized him. But of course she hadn't; he'd been a kid then.

I better get back to work, he said, and she said, Okeydoke, and began to move off, then turned around and said, I mean it, Chip. Don't be a stranger.

I won't, he said. When she was gone with the dog dancing around her, he was too lighthearted to go up the ladder again. Instead, he stripped and dove into the pond, which was still somewhat warm from the summer, and when he got out he sang to himself and worked happily until twilight and went back through the woods feeling quick and alive.

The beer Pearl had promised him tempted him, danced before him, probably because he was here to learn how to live without drinking. He wondered how old she was. Unsmiling, her face could have been that of a woman of fifty or so, but when she smiled, she seemed in her thirties. He'd never met anybody with so much presence. She'd almost frightened him, she was so large and full of life. But perhaps it was situational, the place magnifying something in her. He thought of how Pearl would seem in the city, how he would walk by her on the streets without seeing her; he thought of her on Uncle Charley's sailboat in the harbor and laughed at the absurdity of it, how ungainly and uncomfortable she would be there.

On the third day after he'd seen Pearl down at the far pond, he finished his work early, took a shower using up all the hot water, put on a clean sweatsuit, and jogged over to the great house, up the stairs, and into Bear's closet. His grandfather had plenty of beautiful shirts and sweaters and slacks hanging neatly in plastic bags. In his grandparents' bathroom, he used Bear's straight razor, then his aftershave and hair pomade, and stood back to look at himself. He did not look like the Chip from the last years in the city, not at all. He was tanned, and the physical work from dawn to dusk had made his plumpness disappear; now, for the first time in forever, he had cheekbones. Maybe he wasn't actually handsome yet, he was losing hair at the temples and he looked hungry, but he looked better than he'd looked since those summers as a young man on Martha's Vineyard. He took Bear's oiled jacket and tried on his moccasins, but they were far too large for him. In any event, he liked the way the work boots he'd picked up cheap at the hardware store contrasted with the fine clothes he'd taken from his grandfather, the way they made him swagger a little, like the kind of man who drove a pickup and listened to country music.

As the Jeep curled down the mountain and into the village, his hands began to tremble. He looked for the pizza place he remembered from his childhood, but the slapdash red-checkered sign was gone and he drove past the building where it had once been. When he drove by again, he saw his error; a nice sit-down Italian restaurant had supplanted the pizza place. There was a long and glossy bar inside, and a hostess who looked behind him to see if he was with anyone before she showed him to a little table in the shadows. The place was full, though it was a Thursday night, perhaps because it was the only real restaurant in town.

He looked around but could see Pearl nowhere, and hesitated for a long moment when the server asked if he wanted a drink. At last he said, Just sparkling water, then ordered far too much food to eat at a single sitting, and when he was left alone, he surreptitiously watched his fellow diners, the happy families, the sullen families, the old couples who ate in resigned silence, looking past each other's heads.

His food came all at once: housemade cavatelli, fresh calamari, lemony and crisp asparagus with flakes of Parmesan. A surprise in the middle of New Hampshire. It had been so long since he had eaten with gusto. His body hummed with pleasure. He had eaten more than half the pasta when the chair across the table was pulled out and Pearl sat in it. She wore her hair pulled back tightly and a chef's coat buttoned to the neck.

He put his fork down, and chewed, and swallowed. You're the chef? he said.

Not normally, she said, and explained that her head cook was out with the flu and the sous was off on his honeymoon, and she'd been around long enough to be able to step in. We take care of each other here, she said. You like it?

You're an incredible cook, he said.

You're just hungry, she said. But I'm glad you like it. She smiled, and the wrinkles by her eyes deepened. And I'm glad you took my hint.

Chip felt himself go hot, and drank his seltzer down, and she took a piece of calamari from his plate and popped it in her mouth. No, you're right, that is good, she said through the mouthful of food, and laughed. Then she leaned forward and said, So. Just so you know. I don't play games.

OK, he said.

I think you and me want the same thing, she said.

Oh. Yes, he said quickly, eyes down.

So what's going to happen is you slow down on this food, yes? Take your time. We got another hour of service. I'll send out a tiramisu when you're done eating all this. And when all the staff has gone home, you follow me to my house, yes?

Yes, he said.

Good, she said. So tip like a gentleman. Then she stood and the legs of her chair scraped unbearably on the floor, and she was gone back to the kitchen, and he was alone with the blood pulsing in his ears.

He kept his eyes down because he was sure that the other customers were staring at him, and that they could read his desire on his face. He scolded himself:

She was so much older than he was, she had a huge butt, she was not beautiful, not at all, she was blunt, his sister used her name as a slur, what in the world did he think he was doing. He thought of what his college buddies would say if they saw her; he hated himself for a moment. But the food he could no longer eat was taken away and brought back in lovely Kraft boxes, and a slice of tiramisu dusted with cocoa was set before him, and with the first taste he knew it was no use, that nothing he would tell himself could stop what he wanted to happen from happening.

The bartender and waitresses cleaned and wiped and washed, the last guests wound scarves around their necks and left. He paid his bill, and helped Pearl set the chairs atop the tables, then followed her through the shining kitchen and out the back door into the night. She got into her battered sedan and he followed her through the forest in his Jeep, the trees looming up like ghosts, passing back into the darkness. They came to a stop in her driveway, which he felt vaguely was somewhere near the other end of the town forest. Her place was a tiny antique brick house, very neat. He could just about see the eighteenth-century farming family that had built it frowning out the windows at him.

She opened the door and the little dog burst out of it and peed in a great rush, then pushed its little body back into the house in front of Chip. He expected a riot of colors, overstuffed furniture, tchotchkes everywhere, but Pearl's house was Shaker in its simplicity. Everything was smooth and fine and considered: the long simple cherry table, the walls of books, the smell of chamomile and other herbs. It was warm. The collie curled around his legs in joy, and a black cat slid across the walls and sat, flicking its tail, at the pets' food dishes, which Pearl filled before she even took her coat off.

I stink like a fryer. I've got to wash up, Pearl said. Make yourself at home. She went into the single bedroom, and he sat, petting the dog. He took off his work boots awkwardly and put them under the bench at the mudroom door. There was a hole in his sock that he hid between his toes.

When Pearl came out of the bathroom, she didn't bother with a robe or even a towel. All her flesh shone wet and pink with heat, and there was heat in her mouth when she bent over him, heat in the rosemary-scented water falling in drops from her hair. Stand up, she said, and unbuttoned his shirt, undid his belt, his pants. She was so much larger than he was. She led him to the bedroom. He could not remember the last time he had touched a woman without being drunk. This unmediated feeling was almost too intense to bear. His skin felt tender against hers, her weight pressing down upon him good, her mouth tasting of baking soda. She needed no preliminaries, or she had readied herself in the shower, and she took his cock in her hand, and put it inside her, and held his chest down with one hand as she moved above him.

He had to concentrate very hard to hold off, he had to count, and at last, as soon as she shouted, he let himself go. She cursed under her breath, and used a handful of tissues to wipe herself, then rolled onto her side of the bed. In three breaths she was asleep. The cat came into the room and leapt onto the windowsill and stared at Chip with glowing green eyes. He could make out in the dark the creases that ran from Pearl's nose to her chin, the shock of white in the black hair of her temples. He didn't stir, afraid of breaking the slow, wonderful feeling in him, until his stillness passed into sleep.

When he woke, the sun was in the windows and Pearl had made him coffee, bacon, eggs, a fried tomato. She was in reading glasses steamed up by her coffee at the table.

There he is, she said, putting down her magazine. Bet you're late for work.

Long as the work gets done, I'm good, he said. He felt too shy to look her full in the face. We can, like, go for a walk or something if you want. He thought of the two of them walking in the woods, the little collie springing about, the red and golden leaves, how there would be nobody there to see them and he wouldn't have to hide his face.

Ah, Pearl said. He cut into his tomato, juice spurting. He ate, and she watched him, her face amused, and at last she said, So I'm too old to be beating around any bushes. I'm just going to say it straight up. I'm not looking for a boyfriend or whatever you're thinking this is. You have one job, and you did it, so I think we're good to go. No hanging out. So you go on and eat your breakfast, then you take off. I like my alone time.

She looked like a librarian in her glasses, carefully explaining some cataloging system to him.

Oh, he said, and put his fork down. He felt ridiculous, sorely wounded. He stood quickly and put on his work boots and went across the crisp cold grass to his car. Don't be like that, Pearl called from the doorway, but he slammed his door and pulled out too fast onto the dirt road. The farther he drove from Pearl, the darker his hurt shaded itself, until he was in a black and boiling place, because he was so ashamed of himself, of his desire, because she wasn't pretty, she wasn't young or rich or powerful or educated or smart or accomplished or from an old family, she was just some fat-assed ugly-faced middle-aged spinster from a hick town, she was a fucking nothing, she was embarrassing, and here she was, rejecting him, who was young and educated and his family was his family and he deserved someone better. God, he hated himself for ever having wanted her.

He stopped at the general store. He would never tell his sister what had happened, she would only feel more pity for him, but he felt like a hurtling train and her voice would set him back on track. Her secretary said she was in a meeting, though, and couldn't talk and so he drove to the great empty silence of the estate alone, back to his wordless, bodily exile.

All morning he scraped at the boathouse angrily, gouging the softer wood deeper than he should have, working through a sharp and stinging rain that afternoon, through the windy cold front that set in the next week. And when there was nothing left to scrape, he primed the whole building in one long day, and painted over the course of the daylight hours for the next two, and the boathouse was finally returned to its Victorian elegance, green and gold and gazing in astonishment at its own reflection in the early-morning pond. But Chip could no longer enjoy the place, because Pearl had been inside it with him. He often thought of what he would do if she and the collie came around the pond again, and he had an image of himself kicking the collie right in its apricot mane, in its pink nose, but he knew that he could never do that, he couldn't kick a dog, no matter how much he wanted to kick its owner. His only catharsis was the controlled crack of the rifle, how accurate he was getting from quite a distance away.

When there was nothing more to do on the boathouse, he retreated to the caretaker's cottage, knelt on the linoleum, and ripped it up with his hands, getting cuts all over, finding good hand-hewn pine boards underneath, and thus uncovering his next project. He sat back on his haunches, thinking. He would fix up the caretaker's cottage room by room. He knocked at the wall between the kitchen and living space and saw that it could be opened up into one large room, with the bedroom and bathroom off to the side. He smashed the walls and the cabinets, removed the battered old appliances, and for a few days cooked his noodles and eggs on a plug-in stovetop. One day he rented a sander, and when he was learning how to use it, he felt a presence in the room with him and looked up to find Pearl standing there, smiling at him with a picnic basket in her hand.

What are you doing here, he said. His voice felt rough in his throat, it was so little used these days.

Making amends, she said. Pretty sure I hurt your feelings.

He had to turn away to keep the sting in his eyes from embarrassing him, and when he turned back, he said, I thought you wanted me to leave you alone.

Jesus, she said. I just said that I don't want a boyfriend. I don't think you want me to be your girlfriend, either. It's all good.

With this, the anger faded out of him, because it was true, he didn't want her to be his girlfriend. Now, on the other side of his long, silent rage, he felt foolish.

They sat together on the old horsehair couch. Pearl unpacked mozzarella and mortadella sandwiches on ciabatta with aioli, lemonade, homemade pickles, strawberry-rhubarb tarts. She ate like a hungry man, huge bites she chewed with her beautiful mouth open so that he could see the churn of food inside. He watched, revolted, deeply attracted. They ate everything, even the crumbs, and then Pearl put her hand on Chip's leg.

How's about we agree that whatever this is is just fun? You scratch my itch, I scratch yours. Expect nothing. Keep it quiet, keep it light.

Fine, he said. Her nails were neat, painted pink, her hand heavy. He wanted to hurt her a little. Like I'm your boy toy, he said.

Yeah, she said. Paid in food. And she leaned over and kissed him, and he resisted for a moment, but because her hair smelled like rosemary, and because she was the only person in hundreds of miles who gave the smallest of fucks about him, he kissed her back.

Through early November, they fell into a rhythm. Chip would work all day and drive down to the village at midnight and wait in the back lot for Pearl to come out of the restaurant. Some nights she would bring a box of food to the driver's window and hand it in to him with a tired smile, and this meant that he should go home, eat the food, go to bed; some nights, she nodded in the Jeep's direction as she climbed into her car, and he followed her back up to the house, where she made him an omelet or pasta and they had sex and he spent the night warm beside her radiant heat, the slow near-snores of her breaths. They barely spoke at the breakfasts she made for him, but once in a while she would answer his shy questions. Yeah, she went to college but only a semester and then she dropped out to take care of her dad when he was dying. Yeah, her family was huge, three sisters and seven brothers, and she was the baby, they were all so protective. Once in high school, even, she said, they put a boy who'd been a little fresh into the hospital, got too rough and cracked open his head. She laughed at Chip's face. Don't worry, she said, you don't seem the offending sort. No, I'm a good guy, Pearl, he said. Yeah, that's what they all say, she said, raising an eyebrow, but she let him stay in the neat, lovely house when she went off to work that day, as long as he locked up. Alone, he felt quiet inside, happy, with the dog who'd taken to curling around Chip's feet at the table, the purring cat, the clean white kettle that sang in contralto instead of shrieking, the light softened by the trees all around the brick house, shining through the windows in flitting winglike movements.

He marveled at this place, which, although tiny, somehow held a sort of largeness he'd never experienced before; there was an order, an attention to the exact right thing that spoke to him. It was not luxury the way he was used to it; it was better, it was comfortable.

Over these weeks, Pearl, too, had changed. Chip no longer found her old or ugly, and the qualities that had repelled him now appealed: the heft of her ass and thighs, the frankness of her hunger, the baby talk she reserved for the dog when she came home.

During the hours he worked on the cottage, he fantasized about getting a dog of his own, some kind of sad-faced rangy hound that would accompany him all day and sleep in his bed on those nights he didn't spend with Pearl. But then he thought of moving into Pearl's house one day, and how the imposition of both man and dog upon the careful clean place would be too much, and the specter of his hound dog would keep her from ever opening the place to him, and then he would regretfully return the imaginary dog to the imaginary pound from which he'd adopted it.

He spoke to Elizabeth the Friday before Thanksgiving, and just as he was about to ask what he should do to ready the house for the family, what food he should buy for the meals, she said that there had been a change of plans, their mother would be with Rich's grown kids in North Carolina, Slim and Bear wanted to stay in the Arizona heat, Charley and Diana would be spending the holiday with Diana's sister, and she, Elizabeth, could use a day to catch up on her sleep. But she could come out to the estate and spend the day with him, if he wanted.

He wanted. He wanted them all here, seeing him anew, not as Chippy but as this new person he was slowly becoming. He thought of the boathouse shining unadmired on the large pond, the way he was working fourteen hours a day to make the cabin a sleek, whitewashed little jewel, how he had planned the whole next week to the minute so that he could be finished with the cottage and able to show his family how good he was at this kind of work. How carpentry soothed him, how he'd found in the neat angles and precise measurements something of a redemption. He swallowed. Don't worry, he told his sister. It's just another day.

And she, hearing the disappointment in his voice, said gently that Christmas was only a few weeks away, and this year it was a definite go up at the estate, Elizabeth would make it happen, even if she had to lasso every member of the family and drag them out there herself.

He hung up the phone and stood looking at his work boots until the clerk cleared her throat three times, and he bought a bag of chips and a soda he didn't actually want, and took the afternoon off to go for a hike in the bare chilly woods, because finishing the cottage within the next week no longer mattered so much.

He was still feeling a little flattened at midnight when he drove down the mountain to wait for Pearl outside the restaurant. Though she came over with a box of food, she saw his face and sighed and said, Well, come along then, and he followed her taillights through the darkness to her house. Instead of initiating sex after her shower, she lay down on her bed, and turned on her side, and said, All right, tell me what got you down. She said it so coolly, her voice gave him pause.

And though he was tempted to tell her about his family not coming for Thanksgiving, this would reveal to her who he was, and he wasn't ready to do that yet, to change the balance of power. Someday, perhaps. There were times when, as he worked, he imagined how it would be when she had fully let him in and he told her about his family, and he savored the thought of her face at that moment when she understood that he was more than just a caretaker. She would be startled first, then there'd slide in something like respect for him, a new interest in who he was as a person.

Instead, he said only that Thanksgiving always got him down, since he had no family to celebrate it with.

All the warmth drained out of her face. Are you fishing? she said. Jesus. No, Chip. I cannot invite you to my family's Thanksgiving.

No, Pearl, I— he began, but she went on grimly, saying that she thought she'd made her position clear. They only fucked, that's it. She could never introduce him to her family, just imagine, Jesus, she would never hear the end of it, her brothers would call her a cradle robber, he'd spend all day being mercilessly made fun of. For fuck's sake, Chip. They were not together like that, she thought he knew it.

Yes, he said. I mean, of course. I wasn't fishing, honest.

Listen, she said. I'm too tired to have this conversation. Let's sleep and talk in the morning.

OK, he said, and lay there stiffly as she slept, feeling somehow cheated, watching the cat perambulate in the shadowy room and finally come to rest between their bodies, purring, flexing its paws against Chip's side and piercing him with delicious tiny prickings of its claws.

In the morning, Pearl awoke him with nothing more than oatmeal, although she'd prepared it with butter and brown sugar, and looked at him unsmilingly over her coffee. So, she said. I think we should probably cool this off a little. Just for a week or so. I want you to remember what we're doing here.

You don't have to do that, he said. I remember.

Yes, Chip, yes, I do, she said. Don't come to the restaurant until next Saturday. You hear?

I hear, he said. He rose and put his boots on and as he drove home, his loneliness swamped him.

It was a long week. He felt strange to himself. He decided to fill his free hours by making a built-in bookshelf. There was solace in the steady, careful work. On Thanksgiving, when he went outside for a walk, there was heavy woodsmoke on the air and it seemed to fill his chest, and he found he could hardly breathe. He got in the Jeep without letting himself think and drove past Pearl's house, noting that her car was still in the drive. He parked on the class-six road leading into the town forest, where he could stay hidden, and watched her house. The Jeep ticked itself cool, and crows shouted in the bare branches above. The cold seeped in. When she at last came out with a tower of pie boxes in her arms, and drove off, he trailed her from such a distance that only once in a while did he catch a maroon flash of her car.

Like this they went through the village, over the river, onto the highway. He let a few cars in ahead of him and slowed down when she got off at an exit and followed her two cars back into the old mill town where her family had arrived generations ago, when Italians were not quite white. She drove into a neighborhood that sat between the highway and the river, and parked before a blue ranch with an enormous yard that petered out beyond a pergola and finished at the riverbank. He circled the neighborhood, and then parked farther up the block to watch. Soon other cars pulled up, surrounding Chip on both sides, so many people pouring into the house that he became a little afraid there would be no more room and they'd start bursting out of it.

THE AFTERNOON FELL FORWARD, the shadows spread, people arrived, people left, and suddenly out of the front door of the blue house the children were released in a burst, running in their dresses and suits, some immediately falling and turning their knees green. Someone found a ball, someone found a Frisbee. A set of little girls, all as sturdy and curly-haired as Pearl, stood in the middle of the street behind a larger girl with her back turned, and they crept forward together, paused together, and suddenly sprinted, screaming, as the large girl turned and ran after them and easily caught them one by one.

Watching these happy cousins made Chip smile, but the day had darkened so swiftly into twilight that now the windshield was reflecting his face, and to see his smile on his vague and floating face under his sparse curls, against the vividness and motion of the little girls in their bright dresses, sickened him. He made a grimace and the Chip in the windshield grimaced back. He drove off, and ordered the holiday plate at the diner on the way back, where in each booth sat a quiet old man eating alone, reading the paper and flirting with the waitress when she came by, and in the windows the cold night rolled down over New Hampshire.

As he had watched the blue house, thinking of the warmth and love inside, Chip had decided to let Pearl's deadline go by without his talking to her, to wait an entire week more, and force his absence to make her wonder about him. If Slim taught him anything, it was how to wield silence as a weapon.

Over the week, he finished the cottage. He spent an hour sitting, looking at the place: the exposed beams and clean walls and shining floors, the subway tile and the marble, the windows filled with the slender white bodies of birches. It was a place, he saw now, that he had molded to the simple but complete taste of Pearl.

And then he dreamed of bringing her up there, making a meal with wine and candles, showing her without words what he felt for her. In his mind, he saw her apologizing to him, over and over, kissing him, telling him that she'd made an awful mistake, that she wanted him around. That maybe he should move in with her. Maybe through her he could meet more people, she knew everyone, and he could get work with a contractor, start making real money. And when he lived with her, he could slowly work on her, buying her cashmere sweaters, pearls, modeling manners until she'd accidentally acquired some from him; he'd treat her to a makeover day at a salon to fix the gray hair, introduce her to his friends in the city, eventually even make her presentable for Slim.

On Saturday, a full week after the end of Pearl's imposed exile, he made himself ready. His hands were trembling so severely that he put on too much of the aftershave he'd stolen from Bear, and it was so strong that he had to put down his window to let some of the cold wind blow it off him on his ride to the restaurant. As he waited, it began to snow, a superfine blowing powder that moved restlessly in the air without settling. He had arrived far too early, and had to blow his breath into his hands over and over to keep them from freezing, sharpening his anticipation by imagining how nice it would be inside the restaurant, how good the fresh pasta would taste, how lovely Pearl would look with her face flushed with the heat of the kitchen. He felt he hadn't lived, hadn't even breathed, since he'd seen her. At last, the servers slowly filtered out, then the bartender, the barback, the cooks. When Pearl came out, she was laughing, her face so beautiful in the dim light, and she was calling to someone behind her. He was about her age, a stocky man with a spot of shining scalp in a thick black head of hair. She turned and locked the door, still talking to the man, and they stood there under the light, under the swirls of snow, until Pearl moved toward her car, and the man moved with her. He got in with her. She started up her car, the headlights overbright on the street, and pulled out. She had not once looked toward the shadows beyond the dumpster, where Chip always sat waiting for her.

He counted a slow thousand to himself, then drove slowly up to Pearl's house. As he neared her place, he turned off his headlights and engine, and coasted to the class-six road at the end of the town forest. As he glided silently by, he saw the windows brilliant with light, the dog in the yard sprinting a zigzag through what fine snow had fallen on the grass. And then, from where he'd parked, he could make out very little. He got out of the car, closing his door quietly, and crept through the woods toward the brick house. Pearl had let the dog in, and the sweet thing wasn't in the yard to leap at Chip and dance in joy, which filled him with grief, because he had missed the dog, too, its happy unconditional love. Chip came up to the mudroom door, but couldn't see into the kitchen and living space, so he came around the side of the house to the window, and stood back and to the side for fear that Pearl would notice him.

He needn't have worried; Pearl and the stranger were on the couch, their knees close, their faces nearly touching, talking, laughing, drinking great bulbs of red wine, each fixated on the other. The dog was resting on the man's feet, the traitor. The cat lay on the back of the couch, eyes closed.

Surely, the man was one of Pearl's brothers, Chip told himself, because he had never seen Pearl speak so animatedly, so quickly, so happily. With him, Pearl was guarded, quiet, never a fan of extraneous conversation. But Pearl put down her glass, and touched the man's face, and leaned forward and kissed him slowly. The man put his meaty hand at the back of Pearl's neck. Chip could not look. He bent over in pain.

And then he ran, crouched over, back to his car, slipping on the slick mud of the road, and sat in the Jeep, shaking, sick. Down the mountain again, far too fast. He longed to call his sister, but the general store was closed as he drove by. Back to the estate, heaped huge and black and scornful against the starless sky. Along the drive to his caretaker's cottage, where he'd left the pretty new chandelier alight, in case Pearl could have been persuaded to come to his place. It shone, gorgeously, onto the white yard and into the forest.

AND IN THE HOUSE's warmth he could feel no comfort at all, not in the quiche he had made so carefully and chilled in the fridge, thinking he could feed her for once, not in the shower that he stood under until the hot water was gone, not in the bed with the good Belgian linen sheets and coverlet he'd ordered from one of Slim's catalogs, not in the night, which he passed sleepless and shaking with rage.

He rose before dawn, and paced in the cottage until it felt too tight all around him, the air too stale to breathe. And then he was back in the car, on the highway, driving to nowhere in particular, just driving. He dipped down into Massachusetts, but the state depressed him with its gloomy skies and dead-looking trees and the sad snow-battered houses along the side of the highway, and he could never drive back to Boston and show himself so thoroughly diminished, so he drove for hours along the gray back roads until he found another highway and came back into New Hampshire through Manchester. He found himself in the center of this city he didn't know or really ever care to know; he got out of his Jeep and sat in a cold, denuded park. There were still ducks on the pond, silly creatures that could have flown somewhere warmer and kinder, to some retention pond in Louisiana or Florida full of rich weeds and delicious fish and a sun that came out as promised every day. But, no, they chose to stay for the crusts of moldy bread humans threw them, lazy beasts, and snow would fall on their suffering heads and they would die one night when the temperature dipped below freezing, in a huddle with the other dummy ducks, their hearts stopping one after the other until they were dead.

He was shuddering with cold when he got it in his

mind to leave; the nights fell soon and fast so deep in winter now, and the twilight was already upon him. He hadn't eaten anything in a very long time.

Chip walked into the center of the town, and the scent of food drew him into an empty restaurant where he lingered over a plate of Thai noodles. Across the street, there was a jeweler's with its window decorated for Christmas, a splendid winter-wonderland town scene with laughing pink-cheeked statuettes and diamonds everywhere, earrings glinting off the eaves of the houses like icicles, a glimmering star brooch atop a Christmas tree, diamonds embedded in the tinfoil pond where more pink-cheeked statuettes were skating. He threw down his napkin and some cash and was across the street at the door of the jewelry store before he understood what he was doing.

The jeweler was closing up, but brightened when Chip came in. He was a small and vigorous man, something like an elf, and when Chip examined a vitrine full of rings, he swiftly modeled the larger rings on his own small pale hands, citrine to turquoise to ruby to emerald. But Chip was not such a fool, he would not buy Pearl a ring, he knew that would scare her off for good. He moved on to the bracelets. Some were far too delicate for Pearl's large wristbones, others too gaudy for her taste, but at last he saw a gold band with three perfect sapphire chips set off center, as though they made an ellipsis. He smiled, thinking of the symbolism. At the smile the little jeweler leapt, and nestled the bracelet in a froth of cotton, in a pretty pink box, and tied it with a silken bow and took Chip's credit card and charged him a full month of mortgage payments for his condo, without Chip's ever having fully agreed to buy the bracelet.

Chip was uneasy, but when the jeweler handed the box solemnly to him, he felt that the man was putting hope itself into his hands. The gray cloud that had descended upon him lifted, and everything gleamed and shone all around him, the street itself made beautiful with this new feeling. Outside, the light from a liquor store dazzled his eyes, and he watched as if from far outside himself as he entered and bought a handle of bourbon, and would not let himself think of his sister's disappointment, or of his own disappointment, only of the spicy burn and the warmth inside his stomach. He did not wait until he was in his Jeep to open the bottle, but stopped on a quiet street and held the box with the bracelet between his legs and drank a few great gulps, and his head was pleasantly muffled when he turned the engine on.

Chip drove singing loudly through the dark, drinking from time to time, far too fast, feeling the thrill of the gift that sat like a tiny person in the passenger seat beside him. He thought of waiting until Christmas to give the bracelet to Pearl, but Christmas was still two weeks off, and his family was coming the week before, and with them around, he would not see Pearl, and, well, since he had the courage, he might as well give the gift to Pearl now, get back in her good graces. He checked the time. She would still be at the restaurant, he realized, so he drove to her house, parked at the town forest, and walked down to her house with the bourbon in one hand and the present in the other. He knew she kept her spare key under a rock in the shade garden by the mudroom door, and he let himself in. The dog barked, at first scared, then seeing it was Chip, came out to meet him. He let the dog do its business in the yard, then fed both animals, taking off his boots and stowing them under the mudroom bench, and keeping the lights off.

How strange the house was in the night, he thought, looking around. It smelled the same, of dried herbs and Pearl, it was warm as ever, but without the woman in it, the house was just a house. He went into her bathroom and sniffed her shampoos and conditioners, then came out and lay down on her bed. But just as he was drifting off to sleep, he startled himself awake; she would be seriously displeased to come home and find him already in her bed. He drank deeply, considering. The bottle felt light and he looked at it, marveling how it was already so empty. At last, with a laugh, he understood what he needed to do, and he went into her closet and shut the door on himself, pushing aside her shoes. He would wait until she had showered and was nearly asleep to come out; this was when she was at her kindest, gentlest, most malleable, and he would climb into bed with her, kiss her, and she'd smile in her sleep and curl close to him.

The closet smelled like Pearl's skin and lotion and shoe leather. It was stuffy but nice. Through the crack he could see a slice of light on the bedroom wall as her headlights came closer, then her engine shut off and her footsteps neared, and the kitchen door opened.

She greeted the dog and now there was a flood of light that fell from the kitchen area into the bedroom, but Pearl was still talking; she was, it seemed, offering the dog wine. How strange. No, something was not quite right here, this wasn't the voice she normally used with the dog, and at last he understood with a sick lurch that she wasn't alone. A deep male voice answered. Yes, it said, it would love some wine.

Chip could barely hear a thing then. His whole body was shaking, and his grip on the bottle was so tight he could hardly let it go when the glass began to rattle against the door. He breathed into his hands, suddenly sick with terror. The man he had seen with her was far larger than Chip was, and Chip was drunk, horribly drunk, oh, my god, how had he gotten here, how did he think this was a good idea. He was about to be murdered by that enormous man. He listened to Pearl feeding the dog, pouring the wine, saying she needed a shower, he heard the shower starting, Pearl singing to herself as she showered, and the warm damp steam reached him even where he was in the depths of her closet.

When she came out, she was naked. He saw her rosy flesh as she stood in the doorway of her bedroom saying, Put that down and come here. The man gave a laugh. Now Chip had to hear the wet and dreadful sounds they were making, the slip and grunt of people not himself having sex. He craned his neck but could see nothing but a hairy shoulder. Pearl came, the man came. There were whispers. Then Pearl began to breathe as she always breathed with a little snoring hitch in her nose, and Chip counted to himself, slowly.

At a thousand, he opened the closet door silently and moved through the lightless bedroom, through the kitchen, to the mudroom, where he had forgotten the pink box on the bench when he took off his boots, it had been there all along, shining, perfect, fully visible if Pearl had been able to see it. Small mercies. He gathered the box and the boots up in his hands and carefully opened the mudroom door and closed it and ran in his wet cold socks into the forest far enough so that he could not be heard; then he put on his boots and went shaking back to the Jeep. There was a wetness at his crotch, growing cold. He had pissed himself. He clutched the box in his hands until he was calm enough to start up the car and drive with headlights off past Pearl's house. It wasn't until he was home that he understood at last that he had left the bottle of bourbon and probably the stink of piss in Pearl's closet.

He sat at his kitchen table, petrified with fear. When morning came, and he knew the general store would be opening for the old men who went to get their coffees and cider doughnuts and newspapers, he showered hurriedly and dressed and went down the mountain, and stood calling Elizabeth's home number over and over until his sister was roused out of her deep sleep and angrily answered.

When he heard her voice, Chip started crying. He turned his back on the clerk, on the store with its buzzing lights and groaning refrigerators, the headlines grim about the snowstorm on the horizon. He put his head in the crook of his elbow and whispered, Libby?

Chippy? she said. What the hell. What's going on?

But he couldn't tell her. To tell her would be to see the last of his sister's good opinion vanish forever. So he struggled to stop sobbing, to breathe. By the time he controlled himself, his sister had controlled herself, too.

Whatever it is, it's really bad, huh, his sister said, coolly.

Yes, he said.

OK, she said. Here's the plan. I'll be there as soon as I can. Listen, can you just hunker down? Can you just make it to the end of the day? I've got a deal I absolutely have to finish this morning, it's like years and years of setting up, it absolutely must be nailed down today, but as soon as I'm done I'll have them drive me a hundred miles an hour out to you. Don't worry, Chippy. I'll be there, I promise. Whatever this is, I can take care of it. OK?

OK, he said. He knew she could not.

Don't do anything stupid, she said. Go, like, take a hot shower, and go for a walk or something, all right? And then take another hot shower. Take a hot shower every two hours. You'll be fine.

Right, sure, he said, and hung up, desolate.

He bought an egg sandwich and a coffee and came slowly up the mountain, but when he saw the estate on its hill, his cottage shining in the blue morning against the forest, he knew he needed the mass of his family behind him, otherwise he would be too small against what he felt was coming. He drove the Jeep into Bear's garage, and went through the huge gloomy rooms of the big house until he was in Bear's office, where, in the smell of pipe tobacco and cedar and dust, he felt safer.

Then he sat with a book in Bear's wing chair. The drapes were pulled, but through the gap he could see down the dirt road for a good mile. He tried to read but could only imagine Pearl's morning, her quick waking, washing, letting the dog out, making coffee, making breakfast for the man asleep in her bed. He thought he could feel her shock in his body when she opened the closet door and saw the bottle, the crumpled nest of shoes. When the smell of piss rose to her. He stood in agitation and riffled through his grandfather's desk drawers until he found the secret stash of Bear's favorite Scotch, and he drank it slowly to make his hands stop shaking.

It was almost midday when he saw the first of the caravan of trucks and cars coming up the dirt road, and he steeled himself and moved to the other side of the house, to Slim's blue-gray dressing room, where through her sheer curtains he could watch his cottage. The trucks pulled in and parked around it. Dark-haired men got out, stout and thin, a half dozen or so, and conferred in a knot. These must be Pearl's family, here to threaten him, and he felt a sinking sadness that he had never gotten to meet them, or else they would have known he was a good guy, a gentleman, that he would never have hurt her. One of them went up to the door and knocked and, with no answer, swung the door open and went inside. Then some of the younger men entered, and Chip's great-great-grandmother's books came flying out the door, their brittle leaves spilling, and the few clothes and shoes he had were dumped in a drift, and one of the older men went to the woodshed and came back with the axe, which he embedded in the door.

Then they left, and in Bear's office Chip watched their taillights disappear, and he watched another two hours go by on Bear's office clock until at last he returned to his cottage and saw the plates and cups smashed on his shining new floors, the horsehair couch spilling its guts, his pillow with a kitchen knife pinning it to his mattress. Barbarians. An endpaper ripped out of one of the old books was on the table, someone having scribbled in pencil, Stay off. It was so stupid, so redundant, as though the mess alone weren't enough to warn Chip away.

He picked his things up off the snowy lawn and put them by the heater vents to dry, unwedged the axe from the door, put the pillow and its spilled feathers into the trash, swept up the mess. His head pounded from the Scotch, and he put his mouth under the faucet and drank the cold water deeply until he gasped.

Elizabeth was coming, he told himself. Maybe she was already on her way. She would help him close the house down, feed him, bring him home. But the hours still stretched on endlessly before him, and he went to the utility closet and reached around the water heater, and grabbed Bear's gun just to feel safe in the cottage again. He fashioned a sling out of a piece of old rope and strung the rifle on his back.

Even so he couldn't sit, he couldn't do anything but pace. He hated the cottage suddenly for all the loneliness it had silently held these months, and so he went outside without a jacket or hat or gloves; he would walk fast enough, he reasoned, he would stay warm through walking, until Elizabeth could come. He headed down to the large pond, which had a lace of ice at its edges, and paced around in the boathouse, warm out of the wind; but this place, too, reminded him of Pearl, she had walked through it with her great confident steps, her dog had leapt into the pond after a stick right over there, it was too much. He returned to the great house, and under the angry gaze of painted generations, he stole Slim's most excellent bourbon, the small-batch stuff impossible to find, and gulped until his eyes smarted. Ah, now he felt much better, much stronger.

And as he was going out through the mudroom again, he remembered the pink package on the passenger seat in the Jeep, and he thought that since Elizabeth was going to take him away this very evening, he might as well walk through the woods to Pearl's house, leave the present on the doorstep in apology. Perhaps when she wore it she would think of him. Perhaps she would look at the three sapphires and wonder how he was doing.

What a good decision that was, how lovely this forest was, the soft first falling snow of the storm in the windless tree limbs, how hushed and gentle everything had grown. There were no birds out, no sound at all but his footsteps on the path. A gleam of some late-day light that escaped the low clouds occasionally fell against the far mountains and made them dimly glow. Somewhere out in the woods even the bears were sleeping. He felt excellent, moving so fast, the bourbon having given him courage, the gun solid against his back, just in case; he was ready to leave, he was ready to begin something larger, better, newer, elsewhere.

He saw the distant blush of Pearl's brick house, saw that her car was gone and there was no smoke from her chimney, and thought what a shame, but that of course she would be back quite soon, because the restaurant would certainly be closed early, ahead of the coming storm. It was not even four yet, he had a few hours left before Elizabeth would arrive. He crept near the house and looked in, but all was dark inside, and the dog and the cat must have been asleep together on Pearl's bed because he didn't see them. He balanced the bracelet box carefully on the doorknob where there would be no snow falling upon it, where she would see it as soon as she arrived. He bent low and doubled back along the ditch, hiding his footsteps, to the woods, but once there, in the pleasant warmth, he thought he might wait a little while in case she came back, so that he would get to see her face when she opened the box and saw the bracelet. That was all he wanted: to take that vision of her happy, marveling face with him back into the life he was meant for.

He found a stand of pine so thick that no snow could fall through its branches in this current state of windlessness, and dragged over a log, then sat with his back warm against the largest pine, taking small sips of the bourbon whenever he felt chilly. He occasionally lifted the rifle to his eye to see Pearl's house through his scope. The day darkened all around him as the storm-heavy clouds rolled near, but he didn't notice, as he was already under the far heavier darkness of the trees. The wind rose and the temperature decreased rapidly, but he didn't feel it. He was just so comfortable, and his head was swimming, slowly, and the night was a good one, holding him gently in it. He thought perhaps it would be best if he just took a tiny ten-minute nap. He rested his rifle across his knees, folded his arms, and let his eyes close.

PEARL'S BROTHERS had forbidden her, absolutely, to go back to her house while that closet-pissing creep was still out there. As soon as she saw his little mess, she'd left her place immediately and driven fast to her mother's, seething with rage, but over the course of the day the rage had dissolved, and pity overcame her. Chip probably wasn't so bad, just a lost little rich boy who thought he'd found a savior in her. Oh, these rich boys are all the same, she thought with disgust; of course she had known who he was from the start, he had that same pink fleshy face of all the men of his family, and maybe even she had found it touching that he pretended so hard to be who he wasn't, salt of the earth, scion of nothing, with those ridiculous paint-spattered overalls. So she let him have his sad small lie. Live and let live. But then this morning when she had rushed into her mother's house, and told her oldest brother about how Chip had taken to following her over the past weeks, how, just half an hour ago, she'd found clues that he'd been hiding in her house, her brother had grown furious and loud and called his brothers and yelled at her to stay put. Which meant, of course, that she would sneakily, when they least expected it, do the opposite. Anyway, it was probably true that Chip could use some rough love. Scare him straight back to Boston. She laughed and then felt bad; she hoped they wouldn't hurt him too much.

In the early afternoon when her brothers had all returned to their mother's house, grim and smelling like wind and fire, and they sat down in the dining room to squabble over the garlic rolls, Pearl did not stay put. She quietly put the cat in its carrier and whistled for the dog and went out into the brewing storm clouds and drove the car home far too fast over the abandoned highways, because she had long ago decided that she would never live her life subject to what any man thought she should do.

When she got out of the car in the dark, the wind had risen just enough to drive needles of old snow into her eyes, and she unlocked the door without seeing the pink box, which had anyway fallen into a drift, where more snow would fall upon it and it would lie for the rest of the winter and at last be uncovered by an unusually warm spell in February.

She locked the door behind her, fed the animals, and started the fire with her coat still on, knowing that her power would likely go out when the snow and ice built on the lines.

She blew on the burning newspaper until the kindling caught, and then flames licked at the logs she had chopped herself and stacked against the woodshed. She had water, she had wood, she had candles, she had food. She would be fine for a month, if need be. She was glad she'd come home.

Then Pearl let the quiet of her house seep into her and fortify the most precious quiet at the very center of her. She had not had an easy life; there had been early terror, pain, terrible heartbreaks one after the other, years of ugliness, when everyone thought she was lost. But all that was in the past. She needed other people so that she could make money to live, her body needed to fuck once in a while, but what she really needed was this solitude, deep and impenetrable.

The house was warm now. She took off her coat and turned on the reading light above her head, and the dark forest with the snow spinning fast vanished and was replaced by a dimmer version of her room, the dog, the cat, herself quite rosy in her mother's hand-knitted sweater. She picked up the book that was sitting on the coffee table. For a moment before she began to read, she had a vision of herself as though seen from deep in the forest, an ember glowing in a tiny flicker of light. And of course at this moment Pearl did not think of Chip; she did not wonder about where he was just then, whether he was warming up in the shower back in his cottage; or perched slowly freezing upon a log as the snow whispered all around him and he fell into his longest sleep yet; or whether he was on the log in the night in the snow, raising the scope and thus the rifle to his face in his numb hands, seeing Pearl so whole in her life without him that his body shuddered beyond his control, his pride was touched, his finger moved, and he brought them into a greater darkness yet.

Under the Wave

It came up through the ground in the night. The worst things never wait for sunrise.

She had soothed the bad dream from her little son until he breathed smoothly in the dark and then she crossed the floors to the bed and climbed in without brushing the sand from her feet. The house sat alone in the marsh. They couldn't afford the beach a mile away, and so their consolation was the birds. The great herons, the cormorants, the lit candles of ibis. As she drifted off, she thought of the birds sleeping out in their nests, although by then they were no longer there; they'd already fled.

SHE WAS ALMOST ASLEEP when she felt a great tongue licking the edges of her body, and she opened her eyes to see a bloom of black, her husband's face in a silent shout already moving away, underwater.

And all was stripped from her and all she was was wildness and pain and her lungs bursting in the cage of her chest and her body battered by a hundred invisibilities and the terrible swirl.

Out of the wildness, the branch of an oak plucked her from the water and she clung there, animal, as orange dawned over the marsh made alien with mud.

AND THEN THERE was a span of time that was mostly a low and rolling dark fog. She moved through it, she breathed, but she couldn't say what happened or how or where or why. There was the knowledge of thirst, pain, hunger, only the body articulate.

Images accumulated. A woman in filthy panties limping down a road with a bone knuckling out of her arm. A mass of faceless people huddled around a fire. The gray vinyl of a bus seat, scored like aged skin, and the strange flat brown landscape passing dreamily by the window.

Finally, a warehouse with a concrete floor that was still shining wet with bleach, metal walls that breathed behind her back with the storm that had fallen down on them in extra punishment, a bruised boil of purple sky in the high windows. The survivors poured in and poured in and packed their bodies so tightly to sleep on the bare floors that their breath alone warmed the air. She searched the faces for the two beloved ones, but something told her softly that she wouldn't find them.

She sat in the corner, head bowed. All around her through the day people spoke quietly and wept and some of the refugees with medical backgrounds tended to the wounded, and others passed through sleep and into death. At night, still others turned to their neighbors and fucked as quietly as they could, in desperate affirmation of living.

There were few children in the warehouse and only one baby, who lay rigid in his swaddle and didn't cry.

PEOPLE STIRRED in the morning and went out into the yard and returned when night fell, but she remained frozen. She relieved herself where she sat, but the human reek was such that no one noticed. Another sandwich, another water, another half-hearted fruit, and she sat with the whole accumulation beside her and no one tried to take it. Human decency could still overcome hunger, then.

Late in the night, she opened her eyes to a dim sea of sleeping bodies. She became aware of a darkness creeping through, too large to be a rat, too small for an adult. Cloud unpeeled from moon through the high windows, and in the new light she saw a child riffling among the clothes of others. From the pocket of the woman's sleeping neighbor the child pulled a granola bar and ate it swiftly. Then she saw the woman's lapful of food and reached out hungrily. The woman caught the tiny wrist in her hand and held tight, though the child struggled in silence with tears running down her small pale face. At last she stopped struggling and lay panting beside the woman for a while, her muscles loosening, until the watchfulness fell from her and she was asleep.

The woman let the girl's delicate wrist go and even in the dark saw the bruises already pooling under the skin. She brushed the muddy hair from the girl's face. All sleeping children are as alike as siblings, unformed, soft in the cheek. The woman noticed her sandwiches and ate them, drank the water, ate the fruit, and didn't sleep, just sat staring into the dark until it was light again. Something had begun to vibrate within her.

And when the child opened her eyes the woman looked at her and touched her forehead gently and with a voice gone rusty said, Hi.

Then she stood and the two held hands and picked their way over the sleepers and went out the door and into the dusty yard, first to the ad hoc showers, while the water was still warm. The woman put powdered soap all over their clothes and stomped the filth from them with her feet, then wrung them with her strong arms until they were almost dry. When they went back into the yard, the girl trotted behind her, a good dog. They visited the porta-potties, then they went to the men who were solemnly unloading boxes of food from a truck at the gate. No, the men said, looking away. They couldn't take the woman and the child with them. They had to be registered, they had to wait for the Red Cross to come.

No, the men said for the next five days. On the sixth, the oldest of the men, having carried the weight of saying no to this woman, this girl, who had nothing at all, found his no too heavy to bear and put it down. He sighed and cut his eyes toward the back of the truck. They climbed up. In the roaring dark, the girl light on the woman's lap, they rumbled many miles until they came to a church in a town. The driver opened the door and escorted them into the office of the church, where he found food in the refrigerator for them, and took the collection cash from the safe and handed it wordlessly to the woman.

The girl and the woman held hands in the back of the bus and at each stop shared their food—a hamburger and fries, then a slice of pizza, then a submarine sandwich—and the girl fell asleep with her head on the woman's thigh and the woman's eyes burned as she looked into the quiet fields the bus moved through in the night.

It was dawn when the bus sighed and knelt, and they descended into the city that had been the woman's home. They walked until the girl was too tired to go on, then the woman hoisted her onto her back. The people lifting up the metal gates on the stores looked at these two passersby—the dark woman with her imperious hawk's face, the tiny paperwhite of a girl—saw how scantily they were dressed against the cold morning, and many of them almost said something, but each looked again and swallowed the words, and turned away. The woman carried the girl warm on her back until the streetlights flicked out and the birds began to sing.

By midmorning, they were on the last sidewalk, and the woman set the girl down, then typed the number into the pad, and they went up the stairs and she found the hidden key and they went inside.

The girl saw a look on the woman's face that in the future she would think of every time someone crumpled a sheet of paper into a ball.

Mail was heaped on the floor, and the son's sippy cup from the day they'd left was still in the sink.

The woman undressed the girl and put her into her son's pajamas, then into his bed, and pulled down the shade and turned on the light that shined constellations all over the ceiling. The girl slept immediately.

The woman took a shower that was so familiar in all its details—the heat, the pine scent of the soap, the precise discoloration of the grout around certain tiles—that it seemed to wash away all that had happened to her. When she stepped out of the shower she stepped out of the resolution she had silently come to when she opened the door and saw that nobody had been in the apartment since she'd left it.

The woman woke in her own bed to the girl's thin laugh. She was watching cartoons on the television, and the woman drank a pot of coffee, watching her.

SHE GAVE THE GIRL a good bath and then dressed her in her son's clothes. The girl was maybe two years older than her son had been, but she was sickly and tiny for her age, and he had always been huge, with his parents' great height and muscular build. The clothes fit. She looked decent.

All they did that day was eat, sleep, watch television, buy groceries. The bagger, a bright old man who had always loved to flirt with the woman, said, Long time no see! And she didn't answer, only smiled thinly, because she could never, given a hundred lifetimes, have explained to him the distance she'd come.

The next day, they visited a preschool in the opposite direction of the one the woman's son had attended. When the principal asked how old the girl was the woman, without thinking, said her son's age. The girl grew watchful and sucked in her lips, but she didn't say anything. "My child," the woman called the girl, and the principal looked at this very dark woman and this very pale child and thought about how genes were miraculous and strange, but was afraid of being racist and saying anything. The afternoon was busy when the woman faxed over her son's vaccination forms and birth certificate, and the principal, who had had a day overfull of primary colors and singing, who was thinking already of her cat, her takeout tortellini, her favorite show, didn't read them carefully before filing them away.

The woman showed up at work in a suit on Monday, and people who had vaguely known she was going away said, You're back! How was the vacation? But the woman, who ate lunch at her desk, who never spoke of her private life, hadn't told them where her family was going and they just nodded when she said, Oh, fine. She avoided the break room, where people still talked of the rescue efforts, the ones they knew who had been swept away. One woman who chewed with her mouth open and gave everyone cruel nicknames had lost both of her parents and was given a mental-health month off, and when she returned she was hugged by all with solemn tenderness.

BEFORE, the woman had had a few friends; her husband had family. There was a small, sad wake at a bar that they flew in for. When she disappeared from them soon afterward, they thought they understood her grief, having been swamped by their own, and they let her turn away from them.

It took some time, but the woman understood that the child was funny in her diffident and sideways way; the child understood that the woman was a terrific cook. In the dreamy world of before, there had never been quite enough. But, Eat, eat, the woman urged, and, no matter how much the child ate, the food never ran out.

Mama, the child shyly began calling the woman; and the woman, in return, said Monkey, which had been her son's pet name.

Not long after they came back to the city, the woman took the child to a barbershop and said, Shave it, and out of the masses of pale stringy hair the face emerged, elfin and quick. The child smiled at the new self in the mirror, this bright face with its velvety scalp, the last prettiness gone.

The preschool teachers all thought the child a prodigy, because no other children at that school had ever been so adept or known so many words and numbers at such an age. What detailed drawings! they exclaimed. What extraordinary focus! But the child soon learned that the woman would not look more than once at a drawing with water in it or at anything that hinted of a life lived before the wave. The child began to make pictures of pure lightness—unicorns and suns with grins and houses with fences, the woman's own face in careful brown circles with a giant slash of red for a mouth. Each picture was signed with the name that the teachers called out at circle time, that was written in wooden letters on the wall of the bedroom.

ABOUT SIX MONTHS after they'd returned, while they were walking slowly down the sidewalk on a hot afternoon, the child was dreaming of Popsicles and wind on the skin. There was a red light at a busy intersection, but not in the daydream, and the child stepped out into the street, into the path of a bus. The woman felt a dark horror seep into her and screamed her son's name. The child, who lived in a world with that name carefully written into her clothes, scrawled on the finger paintings still hanging on the refrigerator, paused, then leapt back. The bus swerved in a screeching of brakes and stopped. The driver ran down the steps, yelling with his face hovering only a foot from the child, his cheeks gone purple and spittle shooting from his mouth and onto her. All the sentences he said in his rage were broken: What is wrong with, and I could have killed, and Fucking get your kid in hand, lady.

And the woman's quiet and gentle exterior seemed to break in two and something else emerged that expanded to fill the street. Her face was terrible in its fury and she opened her mouth and curses came out so bitter and fast that the driver shrank and recoiled and ran up the steps of the bus. He pulled off without looking back. The child watched the woman fold into herself and begin to weep. She crouched, pulling the child to her, and whispered that the child mustn't ever do it again. Never. Never. Never risk your life for anything. It is too precious. The woman would die if the child died. The woman would lie down with a broken heart.

They went to a movie then, to sit in the cold and to make their bodies stop shaking, and when they came out twilight was falling on the city. A coworker passed and stopped to say hello. This is my son, the woman said calmly, and rested her hand upon the child's head.

AND SO THEY LIVED, turned only toward each other. The wind blew ice down the city's streets and the trees budded and the lake shone with heat, then it shed the heat in layers and the wind blew cold again. The apartment never changed. There was food in the refrigerator, there were stars on the ceiling in the night. The woman started singing again to herself when she cooked.

Sometimes the child felt a second self inside, a watchful and small and crouching thing. It was different from the child who ate and grew and slept, who walked bravely into kindergarten taller than the other children and already knowing how to read. Hobbies emerged, boys came over for sleepovers, there were remote-control cars and a skateboard under the Christmas tree. The child went alone into the men's room at restaurants and, without having been told, used the stalls there. The edges of the second self were becoming vague. One day it would vanish altogether.

THEN, when the child was eight, they sat eating strawberry ice cream in the shade at the outdoor mall. People went by, slow and squinting in the sun. A man was playing a piano that had been painted purple and yellow and left there for this purpose, and every time he missed a note the woman and her child looked at each other and laughed. The child's head, sunburned under the blond velvet, rested on the woman's strong arm.

Out of the crowd rushed a woman who knelt and looked into the child's face. She was large and soft, with thick yellow hair to mid-arm, trailing other children who looked uncannily familiar. This woman's face wobbled. At first she whispered, then she said out loud a name that made the child's breath stop. Is it you? she said. She said the name again and watched the effect.

And the mother felt the thing that had been vibrating in her for so long cease entirely. She felt the strawberry ice cream drip down her hand, but she couldn't blink or move. Through the skin, the child felt this change in the mother, the stiffening, and was confused.

The kneeling woman started to weep. She took the child's face in her hands and said in a hushed voice, Oh, my god, it is you, isn't it, you look so much like my sister I'd know that face anywhere, no matter the haircut, they never found you in the cleanup, oh my god, tell me it's you. Tell me, talk to me, we thought we'd lost you, too.

The child felt a pain just under the heart, and the

woman's face sharpened and came clear. The children, so blond and slight, gathered around.

But at last the child said in a measured and very small voice, No, I don't know who you are. No, this is my mother.

And then the child said the name that felt right on the tongue, that sounded right to the ear, even though it was a gift from a previous child.

A curtain fell across the blond woman's face, and she gasped and wiped her eyes roughly on her shirt. She stood and backed away, apologizing, saying a little bitterly, Oh, it would have been a miracle if it had been true. She and her children returned to the crowds of people who slowly flowed by. She stopped a few stores away and looked back, but the child would not look at her.

After some time, the child stood and took the melting ice cream from the mother's hand and threw it away, then carefully cleaned up all the drips with a handful of napkins, dipping them in a cup of water and giving the mother's skin a small shock of cold with each touch. The piano player wandered away.

Let's go home, the child said. The mother let her child take her by the hand and lead her away.

Such Small Islands

They came to the summer house in May. There was still a bite to the salty air, and the hydrangeas clenched their fists, wary of blooming. Through the windows, the pool glinted malignantly, and at the edge of the beach, a tiny gardener moved his clipper hands down the hedge. Aura sat under the dining table in the last slab of ocean light as her mother and Phyllis, the housekeeper, spoke in the kitchen. Because her mother was just coming into her glory at work—because Aura was sickly and taxing—Aura's half sister on her father's side was coming to watch her all summer. Now her mother was asking the housekeeper to make sure the girl's bedroom would be ready when she arrived in the early morning. Then, Aura watched her mother carry a glass of wine out to the veranda, where dinner was cooling. She called, Aura! Aura!, the anger growing in her voice, but Aura ignored her. She crept along with the lash of sunlight that swiftly diminished over the floor. The sky bled purplish orange. At last, her mother stopped calling, covered her face with both hands, and gently screamed into them.

In the morning, Aura heard a strange voice in the house when she slid down the stairs in her socks. She came into the kitchen to find her mother at the table in her suit, tapping at her phone with her thumbs. Beside her, a girl with lustrous black hair down to her hips was licking the sugar off the top of her split grapefruit. This was Augusta, but everyone called her Gus. Gus held out her arms, but Aura said, No, you're a stranger.

Silly, of course you know me, Gus laughed. We're sisters. We saw each other all the time before our dad and your mom got divorced. But Aura's mother, who brooked no fools, said that Aura had been only two then, of course she couldn't remember, and their dad barely had time to see her. Then she smiled tightly, as if in conciliation, and said, You haven't been out to the island before? No, Gus said, my mom wouldn't ever let me come. That's right, Aura's mother said, and in her face Aura saw first dislike and then a slow victory, because Gus was here; Aura's mother had won. She loved winning.

Well, her mother said, standing, as they'd discussed

over the phone, she would be gone a lot this summer and there would be times she probably wouldn't make it back to the island for a few days at a time. Phyllis would take care of food and whatever else they needed. Her assistant had sent Gus the information about the Jeep, Aura's medications, the beaches they could go to with their badges; still, for good measure, she handed Gus a thick printout. Be good, love you, she said, kissing her daughter's head. So fast, she was out the door, in the car, gone.

Uncertainly, Aura looked at Gus. She was pretty, Aura saw now. Her lips were thin but she had a smile that spread so broadly it seemed to touch her tiny earlobes, and her teeth gleamed like pearls. Don't worry, we'll figure everything out, little sis, Gus said, and picked her up. Aura pressed her face into her neck and inhaled her marvelous smell, like apples and pine trees and the kind of candies that look like colored glass. That was when something in her began to burn.

The days became bright and smooth. Gus's long limbs browned, her black hair spread like a wing over Aura's face when, in the afternoons, stinging with sun and salt and the tiny abrasions of sand, the girl went down for her nap. There were days of blowsy pink peonies full of ants, bike rides through the golden meadows to the children's beach, coconut sun lotion, Gus in a blue bikini on the pool float when Aura came yawning into the afternoon, rubbing sleep from her eyes. They ate strawberry ice cream watching the sun set over the private beach. Aura refused to go to bed at night anywhere but in Gus's bed, but woke in her own room with the rocking horse in the corner gazing at her with boggled horror. One day down on the sand, as Aura wove strange landscapes out of bladder wrack and eelgrass, Gus sighed and said, This is heaven. She sat up and opened a beer she'd stolen from the fridge and said, You're a lucky kid. Your whole life is what people like me pinch our pennies to have for a single measly week every year. Aura tried to think what this would mean but couldn't. But you are people like me, Aura said. Gus looked at her and smiled. Maybe, she said. I will be.

Soon Aura's mother's absences went from just a few days at a time to four, then five days. Each night when she called to apologize Aura heard the city bleating behind her and felt relieved that she, too, wasn't in the city; that her mother was. It's OK, Aura told her, Gus and me are perfect without you. Gus and I, honey, her mother said but absently, she hadn't even been listening.

By mid-June, they began to go to the beach café to eat dinner once or twice a week, and soon Gus had friends, the boys who had ropy muscles in their legs from carrying trays over sand, the boys who sat at the bar with their collars turned up against their sunburned necks. Gus leaned back in her chair, in her jean cutoffs and bikini top, and laughed up at those who came by to talk to her, and played with her hair and drank the beers they slipped her because she wasn't yet legal to drink in public. When they rode their bikes home through the thick dark she sang songs; and hearing her made Aura feel as though the whole night were somehow bursting out of her, the sleek marshlands covered with darkness, the cobble streets, the giant pale moon, Gus singing and gliding in great smooth arcs back and forth across the dark path, her black hair flicking behind her body.

But one morning as Aura slid thumping down the stairs, there was a disturbance of voices and she came into the breakfast room to find a boy in a pink shirt soft with age, an expensive constellation of holes on one shoulder, leaning close to Gus and murmuring. Phyllis put down plates of eggs before them, shooting spikes out of her eyes. Thanks! Gus said in a strange voice. The housekeeper gave a sniff and went out. The boy saw Aura, and said, What weak, writhled shrimp is this? because at his expensive college he was studying drama. Gus flushed and said too loudly, My little sister!, and opened her arms, and Aura clutched her, hiding her face from the boy. There was a new smell to

Gus's body, a swollenness to her lip that Aura wanted to pinch thin again. The boy was called Oz, short for Oscar, and when he finally walked off, Aura was relieved to have gotten rid of him. But she watched him from the front porch because Gus did, and felt outraged when he went only to the house next door, a giant gray thing with turrets. Gus said, in a low voice, Oh, I like him so much. Aura turned away to make a face. She wasn't surprised when he was back hours later and again they watched from the front porch as he jogged up the drive. Aura willed her eyes to hurt him, his giant limbs, his lacrosse hands, his bare shining chest. He had a fanny pack at his waist with a pen in it for his nut allergy. It seems like that little bag should look stupid, Gus said as though to herself, watching him; but I don't know, he somehow pulls it off. Oz leapt up the steps, palmed Aura's head like a ball, came into the house, and later kissed Gus in the pool for the entire time they thought she was napping.

Now it wasn't just Gus and Aura, it was Gus and Aura and Oz. He drove the kind of car that had no walls, so their whole bodies were terrifyingly exposed to the wind. He picked Aura up and threw her in the pool, though she screamed and kicked and, when she surfaced, wept. During hide-and-seek, he didn't even try to find Aura, just pressed Gus against the pool house while, crouched in the hydrangeas, Aura ripped up handfuls of grass. He was too much, too large, too loud, something about him ate up all the air and left others gasping. After Oz, Aura wasn't allowed to fall asleep in Gus's bed; she was bullied into sleep by that hateful rocking horse in her own room. At the Fourth of July water fight at the center of town, Aura watched, hopeful, as the firefighters turned their great hoses in Oz's direction, but he wasn't knocked down, and when things became too wild, he tucked Aura under his arm as though she were a rugby ball and pushed through the crowds. When she couldn't stop crying at the indignity of being carried like that, Gus said in a hard voice, Looks like someone needs her nap. Aura felt so wounded she was inconsolable, and not even Popsicles would help.

That night in bed Aura chanted in an endless stream all the terrible things of the world that she knew: earthquakes and snakes and broken bones and pinches, car crashes and heart attacks and zits and head lice, and sent the black stream in the direction of Oz's huge, stupid house. But of course when in the middle of the night the noises woke her from Gus's room, they told her that he'd been with Gus just beyond her wall, not in his own house, all along.

The coolness of early summer bled out, and heat

poured into the days like liquid in cups, overflowing into the nights. Aura woke in her bedroom to see a glow in the window and knew it was a bonfire down at their private beach, that Gus had left the house to be down there with Oz and his friends and their booze and music, and that Aura's mother would be angry if she knew. In the dawn, her face ugly in its puffiness, Gus went down with a trash bag that clanked when she dragged it back up to the garage. Aura watched her and saw how the pink flowers were all gone, and now the world was filled with aggressive yellow, tiger lilies and daisies and sunflowers. She heard Gus come up the stairs again, her voice and Oz's murmuring, and then they slept again, long past the time that Aura was supposed to have breakfast. Aura refined her list of terrible events until it felt like a tarry ball choking her. Finally, Phyllis came up with a tray, muttering things under her breath that sounded like curses. Aura ignored the food and lay in her bed alone, her tears so hot they seared her skin as they fell.

At last Gus came for her, brushing her wet hair, a floral dress showing the outline of her body as she stepped through the bands of sun from the windows. Hello, sleepyhead, she said. You slept so late it's almost lunchtime. We're going on a picnic! And she leaned over Aura and dripped her wet hair on the girl's face until Aura loosened her anger and let it fly away. She reached up to Gus's face, the wide smile and teeth, the eyebrows like bird wings, and took her cheeks in her hands and squeezed them until Gus's mouth puckered fishily. The day had been reset. The hydrangeas wore great heavy blue-green globes. The sunlight was honey. Best of all, there was no Oz with them when they rode their bikes to the sandwich shop. Every part of Aura rejoiced that this would be a day like the beginning of summer, slow and clean and soft, just Gus and her, their serious talks and the long gentle silences. But there he was, Oz, waiting at the store with his bare chest and his fanny pack, his enormous feet in his flip-flops. Ahoy, pathetical nit, he said, tugging at one of Aura's braids. She felt the bitter ball rise into her throat again.

Inside, they picked out cut watermelon, beers, a cherry soda for Aura. Don't tell your mom, she hates sugar, Gus said, twinkling. And fun, Oz said, but Gus hushed him. Aura turned away in hatred. She watched the boy in the kitchen making their sandwiches through the vitrine where the salads waited lonely under their shining wrap. The boy made Aura's peanut-butter-and-jelly first, then wrapped it in white paper. When he went to spread the mustard on Gus and Oz's sandwich, he took up the knife that he had used for Aura's, absentmindedly wiped it on a cloth, and used it to spread and flatten and cut. Aura thought of the peanut butter still on the knife, how it was now on the bread. The world came to a sharp point in her. The boy wrapped up the sandwiches, put tape on them, checked them out. Aura watched. She knew. She said nothing.

The ride out to the hidden cove was hot. There was a smashed cat with blood on its teeth at an intersection and it smelled like panic. Oz was impatient with how slowly Aura rode and kept shouting, Come on, pokey, over his shoulder. Aura looked only at the blacktop rushing by and emptied her head of thoughts and made her legs go even slower. At last, they got off their bikes. The ocean was a strange dark blue, and the wind had picked up and was blowing tiny pieces of sand in their faces. They climbed down the cliffs to the beach, where Gus spread a blanket. At this time of day, the beach was in shadow and the caves in the cliffs seemed endlessly deep. Oz kicked off his shoes and dropped the fanny pack and sprinted into the waves, and soon he stood shining with water and saying, Come on, Gus, my sweet. Gus flushed and bit back a laugh and told Aura to make her a giant sandcastle, then took off her dress and joined him, and they held hands until they were past where the breakers crashed, in the smoother waves beyond. Then their heads were close together. Aura knew they were doing that thing again, even though she was there to see them, even though they had left her all by herself on the beach, and she was still a little child and should never be left alone. The hot rage in her grew so large it blinded her. She began to dig with her metal shovel, wildly, like a dog, throwing sand everywhere, on the blanket, on the basket of food, on their clothes, on their shoes, on their cell phones, she dug and dug and hours or even days probably passed, she thought, until she was in a hole so deep her eyes were at water level and there were heaps of sand everywhere. At last Gus and Oz stood over her hole, panting and dripping, saying how incredible it was that such a tiny girl could dig so fast, and such a deep hole, too.

Gus shook out the blanket and unearthed the basket. Oz pulled Aura out of the hole and into the colder wind. She saw with satisfaction that the sand had buried everything, clothing, shoes, fanny pack, cell phones. Lunchtime, he said. I'm starved. Aura stood with a finger in her mouth, tasting salt and sand, watching Gus unpack the forks, the watermelon, the drinks. When she took the sandwiches out, Aura yelled, Not hungry, and ran off toward the caves in the cliffs. Gus called after her, but Oz said, If she wants to be like that, just let her go.

In Aura's cave, the stone was cold and smooth and it was chillier here, though out of the wind. There were seashells heaped in a corner. A pulsing black to her back. Way up the beach, Gus and Oz were tiny, the size of her pinkie finger. She couldn't hear them or see what they were doing. She watched but only out of the corner of her eye. For a long time nothing happened, and the knowledge she'd held like a flame in her dwindled and almost blew out. But then suddenly Gus leapt up. She began kicking frantically at the mounds of sand. She fell to her knees and dug with her hands, she ran back to Oz, she bent over him, she ran off. Oz slowly laid his body down. Aura closed her eyes. The cool rock cupped her, the seagulls screamed, the waves beat a steady time. She didn't mean to but she fell asleep.

When she woke, it was much later, the beach had filled with afternoon sun and shadow, the blanket was empty, and a red light was flashing up where they had parked the bikes. Up and down the beach there were strangers walking along, calling her name. Aura! they called, Aura! But not one of them was Gus, not one wore her hair flicking in the wind, her cool face, her long smile. So Aura stayed quiet, crouched. She was just a tiny thing, after all, at least when measured against the weight of so much rock around her. She was just a little nothing beside the grasping, hissing ocean stretched all the way to the edge of the sky.

Annunciation

Some nights, in my dreams, I find myself running through those hills above Palo Alto again. It is always just before dawn, and as I run I smell the sun-crisped fields, the sage, the eucalyptus. The mist falls in starched sheets over the distant hills, the ones that press against the bay, and I can hear nothing but my own footsteps, my own breath, once in a while a peloton of cyclists whirring out of the morning fog that swallows them up again. I descend, going ever faster through the quiet wealthy neighborhoods, across the empty black river of asphalt that is El Camino Real, then when the road flattens out into Mountain View I am flying, and I see at last the great strong-armed oak that spreads its grace above the whole block. Every time, though, I awaken before I can lift my eyes to the converted pool house, covered in moss and bougainvillea and ferns, which I have not seen in twenty years, and which I won't see again in this life.

My parents didn't come to my college graduation; instead, they sent a dozen carnations dyed blue and a gift certificate to a clothing store for middle-aged women. I would give my left foot to be there, my mother had said, near tears on the phone. But her voice was drowned out by my sisters screaming at one another, the dog barking, and when she put the phone down to stop the ruckus she got distracted and never came back. It is true that one of my sisters had a dance performance that same weekend, another had a soccer match, and another had final exams, and even if these things had been deemed of less importance than the eldest child's college graduation, my two brothers, who were still in high school, could not be trusted to resist having a party in a house vacant of parents.

This was why, after walking across the stage and tossing the mortarboard and hugging my friends, I came back alone to my dorm room, dodging my roommates' families, who were loading all their stuff into cars. I closed the door and looked for a long while at my own neatly packed boxes, the stripped mattress. I took my toiletries, *Moby-Dick* from the box of books, a sleeping bag, a pillow, a hiking backpack full of clothes, and slipped out, leaving everything else behind. I didn't say goodbye. I told no one where I was going. I didn't know until I was outside in the softly setting New England sun that I was turning toward the West.

I HAD BEEN GIVEN my grandfather's enormous Buick when he died, and there was still a packet of his pipe tobacco, a tube of his mustache cream, and a little bowie knife in the glove box. These three things summoned the ghost of him into the car as I drove, and it seemed to me that he was protecting me when I stopped to rest for a few neon-lit hours in a truckers' lot outside a highway strip joint, or when I cruised some small-town grocery store for the cheapest and most abundant calories. I had only a pocketful of change and a half tank of gas when I rolled around the curve and saw San Francisco in its dark glitter before me. I'd visited libraries along the way to check an internet bulletin board, where I had advertised the Buick for sale, and it happened that I arrived an hour or so before I had agreed to meet the car's buyer in a hospital parking lot. I pocketed the bowie knife, and felt a pang that I was trading my grandfather's ghost for a paltry thousand dollars in cash, but told myself that surely the dead desire the living to eat.

For a month, I had the upper bunk in a Chinatown youth hostel, a life swept clean of family and friends, an emptiness that I could fill in whatever way I wished. I wished to go hungry until dinner to save money, to walk the hills of San Francisco, asking at every bookshop and bar for a job. Nothing was available, at least not for me. When I squint back through time, I can see her again, this restless, ill-clothed, stringy-haired, half-starved girl who could not, for shyness, look a bookshop manager in the eye.

At night I lay in my top bunk, listening to the two shiny Brazilians assigned to the bottom bunks as they pulled their mattresses to the center of the floor and had gentle, wet, endless sex. Once I had to go to the bathroom, and when I tried to climb down soundlessly a hand grasped me around the ankle, and a voice from below invited me to join them. In the bathroom, I stared at my face in the mirror, trying to see if the new person I was becoming was someone who would have a threesome on the floor with Brazilians so beautiful it was hard to see their faces for their glow. I decided that I would instead be a person shivering in her pajamas on the disgusting puce couch in the common room. I regret this decision, as I regret all the times in my life that I turned away from living.

My money was dwindling, and I submitted my résumé to a temp agency. I went in on a Friday to take a typing test, and before I left I was offered a job all the way down in Redwood City, starting on Monday.

For hours in the library afterward, I scrolled the internet bulletin boards for a place to stay, and when I had almost given up I saw Griselda's ad for a converted pool house in Mountain View. The rent was cheap, because the renter was required to do assorted daily chores, some, Griselda admitted in the ad, unpleasant. Men were preferred. I ignored this last bit and took a bus south, and walked a mile, and saw the cottage for the first time in a kind of spectral dusk. The place sang to me in a register straight out of the fairy tales I'd loved as a child. It seemed a place built for Titania and Puck and little volatile men who grant three wishes.

There was an enormous dog guarding the gate of the big house, an English mastiff of more than two hundred pounds that opened its mouth as if to bark but gave only a series of dry coughs. Griselda had had his vocal cords removed, she would tell me later. She looked astonished when I said that seemed cruel, that it was like taking away a human's ability to speak, and she responded that this was nonsense, that of course dogs couldn't speak. Also, surely, she said, it was less cruel than kicking him when he barked too much. I rang the bell outside the gate and waited, then rang it every five minutes until finally the door opened and a shadowy figure emerged who pulled at the dog's chain until he backed up, then looped it around something so his orbit was small, and at last she stood before me, peering out the gate.

I had never met a person like Griselda in my life. She was as tall as I am, rather tall for a woman, but I saw her as a strangely wizened child. Her blunt inky bob was held back on one side by a plastic barrette, and though her face was round, its skin had wrinkled into a topographical map. Her eyes were sunken, their positions vaguely semaphored by eyeliner that fell in crumbs down her cheeks. Her neck was extremely long and her body, in descending, swelled ever outward from her fragile shoulders until it ended in two purple ankleless columns overflowing a pair of cracked patent-leather slippers.

Who are you? she said. What do you want? I heard even in these few words her German accent, which also seemed like evidence that she belonged to the world of the Black Forest, wolves, dark magic.

I told her that I was there to rent the cottage, that I was quiet and responsible and punctual. I handed her my résumé through the gate. She did not take it but looked at me for a long time and told me that I wasn't a man. I said that I knew I wasn't a man, but I could do whatever a man could do, that I was as strong as a man, which certainly wasn't true anymore, after my month of starvation. Griselda sighed.

Ah. So she is a feminist, she said. I was a feminist once. But then the robbers came at night. And there was no man here. And they tied me up and took everything I had that was good.

This gave me pause; in the pause, I saw the little house suddenly begin to slip away from me, and so I said, What, they even stole your feminism? Then she blinked and her face widened; it was a miraculous sort of unpleating, and she laughed a large, loud laugh and clicked her tongue, and said, Well, yes, fine, fine, fine, you take it. I don't know why but I like you.

Tonight, I said, quickly, and held out the roll of cash that was my entire worldly fortune, save twenty-three dollars and sixty-four cents, which had to keep me until my first paycheck.

She sighed and took the cash and removed the key from her key chain and put it in my palm. Tonight, fine, she said. Tomorrow you begin with the chores. Gladly, I said, and without even looking inside the cottage I ran back to the bus stop, rode it northward, sprinted uphill to the hostel, packed my things, spent a second in the kitchen considering, then threw into my backpack the dustiest of the pasta and rice and ramen and cans of beans and bulk boxes of Chinese green tea and the crusty oil and salt and pepper, all things that other hostel dwellers had left because they wanted them to be used, I reasoned, knowing, even as I stole this food, that I was beyond the pale.

The cottage was cloaked in darkness when I returned. I opened the door, and the place seemed to embrace me. I didn't turn on the light. I saw sharply outlined by the moonlight a woodstove, a kitchenette, a shower and toilet behind a glass wall. Best of all, stretching across the entire ceiling there was a vast skylight, showing the huge oak's muscular branches and the stars sharp between them.

I went out the back. I found that Griselda's pool had been filled with white gravel that glowed in the moonlight, and that the roots of the tree made a smooth and beautiful stool and table. There was a sound inside the tree like a soft, low, constant hum, which I took to be the movement of the tree's sap in its immensely slow circulation, or its long and meditative respiration, or even the way the tree sang to itself in its gladness at being so strong and so alive on a chill bright night like that one.

Inside the cottage, of course, there was no mattress, only my sleeping bag. I slept on the carpet and woke in the morning to a shower of light falling through the oak branches, falling warm and good upon my face.

Griselda's tasks for her renter were, as advertised, unpleasant. She showed me how to unlock the gate, how to fill the food and water bowls for the mastiff, how to scoop up the huge quantity of poop he left on a strip of Astroturf at the end of the range of his chain, and how to spray down the acrid expanse until the smell and the flies were somewhat mitigated. The dog watched me from a bamboo thicket that was pressing itself against Griselda's sprawling 1960s ranch house. It was a ramshackle place in this neighborhood of neat and lavish mansions. I was also to scrub the dog down once a month or so. Griselda said airily, waving her hand, He stinks! And though it was true that the dog needed many consecutive washes to stop stinking, he and I looked at each other and tacitly agreed that I would not be the one to bathe him. He weighed far more than I did and his teeth were long and yellow.

Why, I ventured to ask, when I was safely away from him, watering geraniums in the giant pots in the courtyard, was the dog always on a chain?

But instead of answering, Griselda sat down in one of the wrought iron chairs she had scattered there and asked me if I knew that she was the daughter of an industrialist in Germany. Very, very wealthy. Pins! Some kind of pin nobody else in the world could make. When she was a child, every Christmas Eve, after the department store in her town closed for the night, it would open just for her, little princess Griselda, and she was allowed to run up and down the aisles and choose any toys she wanted. How magical it was in that empty store, with its sweet evergreen boughs and oranges and the smell of Feuerzangenbowle in the air!

I listened, thinking it was odd that when Griselda spoke, she seemed not to be telling a story but rather to be reciting something that she had memorized verbatim.

Perhaps, I told myself, she loved to tell stories to create a past she never had. And who was I, who had just erased my own past, to blame her for this.

It took me two hours to finish my chores that first day, and would take me an hour every day from then on. When I was done, Griselda hefted herself upright with a grunt, saying, Wait, I have something for you, and disappeared into the house. She came out with a huge jar, the size of a human head, half-full of honey.

A sin what my wealthy neighbors throw out, she said.

Wait, I said. You found that in the trash?

Well, yes, she said, but don't worry, it is not poisoned. I had some in my tea this morning. And look at me, I am still alive!

That Monday, there were twenty temporary workers like me assembled in the conference room of a squat, despondent yellow brick building that was the Department of Human Services in Redwood City. We had been hired by a consultancy firm to help digitize and streamline the social workers' files on each child in the system. I hovered near the bagel table during the orientation PowerPoints so that I could slip as many bagels as possible into my backpack, each a whole meal I wouldn't have to buy. In the shadows on the other side of the table, there was another woman poaching the bagels, and I disliked her immediately, partly because she kept snagging the ones I was about to take and partly because she offended my aesthetic sense. She had long pale unkempt hair to her waist with a fuzz of dandruff in the center part, a strange orange tint to her lips and fingernails, and was wearing an avocado-and-tan-striped high-necked shirt-and-skirt combination that would not have been fashionable in the seventies, when it was first imposed upon the world. Her glasses were enormous, with yellow lenses that darkened when she stepped outside into the sun, and that gave her a cagey look in any light. There was a thick funk to her that reached out to me even across the table. Anais, she had written on the name-tag sticker on her chest, though she looked more like something biblical, a Judith or Esther or Hagar or Zipporah. A prophetess, a martyr, a believer who loved the ache in the knees after a long session of prayer.

When in the afternoon we were paired off with sample folders, each containing a fictional child's case notes, so that we could practice either keying in answers to an online questionnaire or creating a five-hundred-word narrative of the child's life, I watched with growing unease as all the people I wouldn't have minded being paired with went off together, until in the end I was left with Anais.

She sighed, looked me over with narrowed eyes, and said, Ugh, all right.

All right, I snapped back, though being her partner was not in the least all right.

We sat side by side at our paired computers. She blazed along with the data entry, but because I was vain about my writing, I was so slow with the narrative that I was only a few sentences in when time was called.

Anais leaned in to read what I had written, and I held my breath and tipped myself away from her smell, and finally she said, No, no, this won't do. You're being too fancy. You got to be simple, clean, in and out, get it?

I must have looked as stung as I felt, because her voice softened. She said, You got to understand. We're about to see some pretty heavy stuff with these kids. Neglect and hunger and rape and broken bones and a bunch of other bad stuff, and if you're writing all that fancy prose you're going to feel all that badness in you. But if you're sharp and cold it won't get to you so deep. You see what I'm getting at? You need to protect yourself, sweetie.

I have always had difficulty with tenderness that comes to me unexpectedly. Perhaps it was also true that by then my beautiful solitude had slid a little into loneliness. My eyes filled with tears. Anais leaned even closer, and put her hand, stinking of something strange, on my face and said, Oh, sweetie, you'll be OK.

When we were given our first real folder to process, I saw that Anais was right: The child in it had a life that was relatively good compared with many we would see, but still, a great horror radiated from between the lines. There were many different social workers' notes documenting the discipline problems of this small boy, the diagnoses and medications, the cycling into and out of foster homes, all the way back to the initial trauma and the separation from his mother, who had been deemed unfit because she had left her baby with a paramour who had somehow broken the little boy's leg. I wrote my narrative as quickly and cleanly as I could, then, while Anais was finishing the online form, went to the bathroom to cry. But once I stood there in the stall, resting my head against the cool metal, I couldn't. Something was stuck inside me, huge and uncomfortable.

When I returned to my desk, I understood where some of Anais's odor came from. She had taken a small container of orange powder from her battered pocketbook and measured out a careful spoonful. I watched, astonished, as she swallowed the powder down, staining her tongue and teeth orange. Turmeric. It's my medicine, she explained, daring me to say something.

Witnessing this only added density to the enormous immovable object inside me. When I got home to the cottage, I had the idea to put on my running shoes and go out into the delicious coolness and try to run the bad feelings off.

I went through the expensive streets of Mountain View in the dusk, and though I could not yet run far, and I still couldn't cry, the lump inside me dissolved enough that I felt relief.

I returned to the cottage to find a gift from Griselda

outside my door: a beautiful armchair. On the note, in a spiky and elegant hand, she wrote that she had noticed I had no furniture yet in the cottage, and that someone like me always needed a separate place to sit and think.

The following months became a plait of four strands: the dark horror of my job, with all those damaged children who burned beyond their folders into the world at large; the increasingly long and ecstatic runs I began to take every night after work; Anais, my coworker; and Griselda, with her stories and her gifts of rescued castoffs.

One morning, as I scooped up dog shit, Griselda told me that she had once been a model in New York in the 1960s. She showed me a torn-out magazine photo of a dark-haired woman who, except for the extremely long and elegant neck, looked nothing at all like her. She said that back then she went to parties all the time, really scandalous parties, and she knew everyone—Lou Reed, David Bowie, Andy Warhol. In fact, she had been in a sex film of Andy's. But under an assumed name, of course.

Oh, of course, I said politely, scooping, scooping.

But as much as Griselda spun her stories around me, Anais, who had begun to interest me, was resolutely silent. She had pinned above our shared desk a photo of a tiny child of three or so, with long red braids on either side of her face. She was so striking that I had to mask my surprise when Anais told me that the girl was her daughter, and that her name was Luce.

Afterward, I glanced at Anais's face surreptitiously throughout the day, seeing this woman whom I had believed to be a spinster, or uninterested in sex, suddenly as a mother. I was so young, with the distorted vision of youth, and had assumed from the way she dressed that she was much older than me. I saw now the dry skin of the emaciated where before I had seen wrinkles. I saw a young woman wearing the thrift-store costume of a much older woman. I began to sense that she was hiding something.

We were, finally, given our first paycheck. At last, I had enough for rent and food; the extra left over felt luxurious. I began to buy fruit from a food cart to supplement my peanut-butter-and-jelly sandwiches at lunch, a little clamshell of beautiful fresh strawberries and watermelon with some mint sprinkled in. There was a kind older social worker I sat with in the sun while I ate this fruit, a comfortable woman named Shelley, who talked about her grandchildren and the weather and books. During those months, Shelley became a good acquaintance, if not a friend. I had no friends. I wanted none.

One day I felt the joy of my extra money and bought

a second clamshell of fruit to take back to Anais, who, as far as I could tell, only ever had soup she sipped from a beige plastic thermos.

I handed it to her, and she looked at me, wary of my gift, then a softness settled into her shoulders and she said a quiet thank-you, and ate the fruit slowly with little grunts of appreciation, saving half of it to take home to her girl.

After that, things were more balanced between us. I had grown used to her turmeric-swallowing. She grew comfortable enough with me not to hide that as she worked she was listening to the voice of an evangelical minister in her earphones. I had heard of this man. My roommate in college, a former evangelical, spoke scathingly about him, calling the minister a charlatan and a hypocrite and a serial seducer of young boys. I had committed to my dispassionate life, though, and didn't mention the rumors to Anais. Who was I to ruin her pleasure in this form of god? I liked it even when, once in a while as she listened, she nodded with a radiant smile on her face.

SOON SHE BEGAN to use the landline in front of me, which we weren't allowed to use—it was for the actual social workers, who resented us—to talk to the mechanic who was always fixing something or other, carburetor, hose, tire, on her Vanagon.

Vanagon? I asked. She smiled, then seemed to make a decision and took her wallet out of her pocketbook, and from it pulled a photo of a boxy olive-green Volkswagen van. My home, she said proudly. I bought it cash, and so I don't have to pay rent. It's got everything, a bed my girl and me share and a table and a little kitchenette and a toilet, but the shower's broke and I'm saving up to fix it. We can up and go whenever we want. Say there's another earthquake, which there will be, mark my words, all we do is get in the Vanagon and drive to somewhere safe.

Then she seemed to regret having said this much, and to all my questions afterward she frowned and shook her head.

I am sure I would never have discovered what Anais was running from if I hadn't come back from the bathroom one day to hear her on the landline, pledging a thousand dollars to the evangelical charlatan's overseas ministry. I must have let out an incredulous sound, because she looked at me and made a furious face. She said that she would send a check, and slammed the receiver down. Then she stood up, quivering with rage, and said loudly that it was her money, she could do whatever she wanted with it.

All the other temps stopped working to look at us. I said, You're right.

For the rest of the morning, Anais typed on her keyboard so hard that I was afraid she might break it.

This was our six-month anniversary of the digitizing project, and we were, surprisingly, over our quota. Our supervisor, a sweaty new college graduate who looked like all the frat boys I had gone to school with, celebrated our achievement by buying us a stack of pizzas and a sheet cake. He also forgot where we were and the gravity of what we were doing, and brought a couple of twenty-four-packs of cold beer.

I watched from across the room as Anais stood silently in a knot of people, sipping a beer so fast that it was clear to me she had never in her life drunk one before. I don't think she would have had one now if I hadn't upset her so deeply that morning. I watched with dismay as she opened a second beer. This she drank even faster, and I watched her give a little burp into her fist, and the people in the ring around her all at once leaned back, perhaps because of a sudden waft of spice.

There was a speech I didn't listen to; I was watching

Anais wobble, her eyes grow a little loose behind her thick lenses. I made my way around the room until I was standing right behind her. The speech ended, everyone applauded and began shuffling out of the conference room, and I caught Anais's arm as she made to move but tripped on nothing and started to fall.

She looked at me. Uh-oh, she said. I steered her into the bathroom so quickly that I was able to pull her hair back into a bun at her nape before she vomited into the toilet.

She retched and retched, neatly, like a cat, except for in the first torrent, when some puke had splashed back up onto her chin, her glasses, and the high seventies bow of her shirt. She sat, bleary and sweating, on the side of the sink while I wet a paper towel and wiped her face, then ran her glasses under the water and tried to clean the bow by dabbing it with a fresh towel. I saw that it attached to the collar of her shirt with a series of tiny buttons all the way around, and began to unbutton them one by one.

She watched me. Without the glasses obscuring her face, she looked young, my age. She was not unpretty, I saw with surprise.

I undid the last button, and took the end of the bow to pull it open, but she put her small hand over mine, squeezed, and looked me in the face. Then she pulled the end and the bow fell away. Her neck was scrawny and pale. Across it there was a raised purple scar that stretched from beneath one ear all the way to the other.

Almost killed me, she said. Luce's dad.

I saw then why she was so wily, so secretive, why she lived with her child in a van, why the ability to escape trumped every other need.

So now you know why nobody gets to tell me what to do ever again, she said.

I thought about what to say while I washed out the bow with hand soap and hot water, then held it under the hot-air dryer. The fabric was shiny, synthetic, thin from wear, and didn't take long to dry. I had found nothing to say by the time I began buttoning it back around her collar.

Gently, I tied the bow in a great loose loop that swallowed up Anais's angry scar.

Then Anais leaned forward and kissed me gently on the lips. She tasted like turmeric and beer and vomit, and I moved my head away.

But, as I did, her face changed, a horror entered it, and she snatched up her glasses and ran out the door. I spent some time cleaning up the bathroom. When I came out, she had left a note on my keyboard: Sick. Forgive me. Won't happen again.

I didn't get to tell her that it was all right, that

though I didn't want it to happen again, either, I didn't mind that it had taken place once. By the next day Anais had built such a strong wall around herself that I was never going to be able to reach her again. Not once during the next few months did she speak to me about anything other than work-related matters. I tried to get her to talk about Luce, but she wouldn't. She was gone, closed. I had done some violence that I wasn't at that time capable of understanding.

As the silence between us grew, I began to be unable to sleep at night, thinking about Anais's girl. Every day, her little flower of a face looked down at me from the photo above the computer; when Anais was in the bathroom or slowly measuring out her turmeric, I would look at her and think about how Anais sent her money to that disgusting evangelical charlatan. And then I would think about the Vanagon that she could never keep running properly, and what would happen if Luce's father found them when the vehicle was going through one of its many sulks. If they would be able to get away from him. If Anais would be too holy to fight him off if he were to try to murder her again.

After a while, I had thought about Anais and her daughter so constantly that I grew angry. It began to seem wildly irresponsible for any mother to waste her money on religion and vehicle maintenance, to fritter away the means by which she could get an actual apartment, not a box on wheels, to choose not to build up a safety net to protect her child. There was only a flimsy aluminum door between the tiny girl and all the danger in the world.

As if sensing my anxiety, one weekend Griselda told me a story about her life. Once, she said, in the 1980s, a very wealthy lover got so mad at her while they were on his yacht in the Caribbean that he slipped her a mickey, and when she woke up she was floating on a raft out at sea, sunburned and wearing only a bikini. She floated like this for a week or so, lost in the blazing sun during the day and the stars at night, surprised by two sudden rainstorms that put enough water in the bottom of the boat to keep her alive, circled by sharks, until she thought that she would simply jump into the waves and let the sea take her down into its hungry depths. But then she was rescued by a family with a sailboat whose father had wanted to write a book about their year on the seas. They thought they'd caught a mermaid! They carried her to a hospital in the British Virgin Islands, where a doctor fell in love with her, but she had to break his heart and go back home to her daughters, who were teenagers and hadn't even realized she was gone.

That sounds like a difficult experience, I said, as neutrally as I could.

Oh, indeed, that was a very bad experience, Griselda said contemplatively. But, once I was out of the hospital, the hush money from my lover who had made me a castaway was excellent.

And she smiled her wide, gorgeous smile that was like an explosion in her face.

One Friday, after Anais gave a curt little nod and said, Happy weekend, and slung her pocketbook over her shoulder, I followed her, though without at first meaning to. We were going in the same direction, and I simply continued on past my bus stop, drawn almost against my will. She walked with her martial step through the scorching streets of Redwood City, probably not wanting to spend money on bus fare. I stopped, watching from behind a tree, as she entered a cinderblock day care, and came out holding the hand of her daughter. She was smiling down at Luce, and the girl was talking excitedly up to her. They walked slowly for a few blocks to a library, and I lingered at the window of a convenience store across the street, pretending to agonize over a rack of gum, until they came out again, the girl with a book tucked under her arm.

I followed them as the road twisted into a copse of bay laurels and cypresses, where I saw the Vanagon hidden by the thick shade. There was the flicker of a kerosene light in the window. I saw that the night had begun to deepen. There was the smell of cooking—garlic and some kind of starch, like pasta. But seeing the dark forms of Anais and Luce moving in the light made me ashamed of myself, and I quickly left the copse. In self-punishment, I walked the three hours back home.

This should have been the end of it. I should have let the distance sit between us. But I had not yet learned wisdom, and silence had not yet sunk into me as deeply as it later would. That week, I was sitting out in the noontime sun with the social worker, Shelley, eating cut fruit with mint, and talking about Anais, about Luce, about the Vanagon.

Just between you and me, I confided, I think she's an excellent mother, but I'm worried about her daughter. I think it's not impossible that she doesn't take the girl to get her shots. The preacher she listens to doesn't believe in vaccines.

And Shelley nodded slowly, smiling, which at the time I took to be agreement with my assertions of confidentiality, but which I came to understand did not commit her to anything like silence, or discretion, or inaction.

I ask myself now if some part of me wanted Anais to

be jolted; if I wanted, obscurely, to force her to find a solid place for her child. If I knew that she and her daughter might be separated, I would never have put it like this to myself at the time. There are moments in our lives when our sense of our own goodness is so shaky that we build elaborate defenses against the possibility that we may be far worse than we fear. I have come to think that I had a secret intention, held at the very center of my actions, so small and dark that I pretended not to see it then; I could not see it even a decade later. It is only now, when I know myself to be good and bad in equal measure, that I can glimpse it, if barely.

As I took care of the mastiff that weekend, Griselda sat in the courtyard in a plastic chair, soaking her feet in a tub. She was telling me another of her tall tales, this time about the period when she taught philosophy at Princeton, back in the seventies and eighties, and had an affair with Derrida—or was it Nagel? It's astonishing how things get confused as one ages, she said. I filled the water bowl, half smiling at the idea of Griselda as a philosopher when her thinking was so muddled she couldn't get her lovers straight.

Then she said, with her eyes closed and her face turned up to the sun, In those years, I felt the world stirring within me. I was so alive then.

I turned off the water, and said, quickly, Yes, that's exactly how it is, exactly. I told Griselda that I had felt that way ever since I moved into the cottage eight months ago. Every day, I sit with my tea out under the oak tree, I told her, and I press my ear to it and hear the way the world and the tree seem to have found a resonance within me. It is like a triangulation—the world, the tree, and me.

Then I saw a bee land on the chair close to Griselda's bared shin, and I said, Careful, bee.

She bent and looked at it, then looked across the yard, at the geraniums, where more bees were crawling in and out of the vivid red flowers.

I watched as slowly her eyes lifted above the wall of bamboo, to the top of the great oak tree, and she held her hand in a visor and squinted, looking there for a long time, frowning.

When she dropped her hand, in her face there was something like pity. Ah, she said. I'm so sorry. It's not the resonance of the world, or whatever you think it is. It's bees.

I couldn't believe that I had missed them in their thick orbiting of the top of the tree, where there must have been a hollow. Griselda forbade me to go into my backyard, saying that she was sorry, there were legal issues. One of her former tenants had been stung and had an anaphylactic reaction and had to go to the hospital, and now she was bee-shy as a landlord—she couldn't afford such hospital bills again!

She brought me a gift of six beautiful amber-colored drinking glasses in apology, so that I wouldn't have to drink out of old pasta-sauce jars anymore, and that night I sat on the cold woodstove to drink my tea from an amber glass, and felt a longing to be next to the tree as usual.

I woke on Sunday morning to a feeling that something was wrong, and stood blearily in the shower, trying to understand what it could be. At last, I lifted my eyes to look through the skylight, where, at the top of the tree, a man had belayed himself and was spraying the hive, a can of chemicals in each hand. At the moment I looked up, he was looking down at me, but was oddly faceless, which I couldn't understand until I had screamed and cowered on the floor, and crawled naked out of the shower, and thrown on my clothes and run out into the driveway barefoot, my hair dripping.

Griselda was standing colossal there, supervising the spraying from below. Oh, don't worry, she said. His name is Gabriel, he does handiwork for me sometimes.

Yes, unfortunately he did have to spray at this time in the morning, she said. It is when the bees are sleepy and won't sting so much.

Yes, he has a face, she said, I just made him wear three pairs of my pantyhose over his head to protect himself.

And at last she said, impatiently, Ah, Liebchen, he doesn't care for your nakedness. He is up in a tree being stung by bees.

ON MONDAY MORNING, the tree did not hum its happiness.

At work, there was no Anais. She did not come in, did not even call to say she wasn't coming in, my supervisor complained. My cubicle felt lonely and the face of the little girl looked down at me, an accusation there.

When after work I walked all the way to the little grove of laurels and cypresses, the Vanagon was, of course, gone. There was an indentation in the soil in the shape of Anais and her child's life.

The next day, though I stood outside the day care and waited to see her, Anais did not come to pick up her daughter, and the women finally locked the door. It was clear that the child had not come in that day. I grew so concerned, I could hardly sleep.

After a few days of standing on the street, watching, I summoned the courage to go into the day care, which smelled like paste and piss and crackers, and asked the lady in charge about Luce and Anais; a window slammed shut in her soft face, and in Spanish she called the other two child-minders over and the three of them stood in a ring around me defensively, saying that Anais was gone, that she did not want to be found, that I had better forget her.

The state had come around asking questions, the lady in charge said. I wasn't someone sent from the state, was I?

Oh, god, no! I said. I am not a threat, I wanted to say. Then I understood that to any woman on the run the fact that I was there, trying to find her, meant that I was indeed a threat.

And so I began to come home from work directly, to change into my running clothes as quickly as I could, and I would go out into the late afternoon and twilight and night, trying to spot Anais's van in the towns all around Redwood City, my heart lifting every time I saw an olive-colored van, and crashing down again when I understood that it wasn't Anais's, that she had gone somewhere too far for me to run to.

I BEGAN TO RUN farther and farther at night, in expiation, but also still looking for her.

I am so sorry, I wanted to tell her. I am not someone you need to run from. I would never harm you. I would never ask the authorities to take your child from you. You do not need to fear me. But she had gone somewhere out of reach of my contrition.

A month passed, and then another. My body had become whittled with all the running. The bees came back, and I didn't tell Griselda; I just sat in the chilly bright mornings drinking my tea and listening to the low song inside the trunk. I took care of the mastiff before work every morning. Some days Griselda joined me and told impossible stories from her life, and other days she would leave a gift on my doorstep: a bottle of hot sauce, an expensive face cream, barely used. The only thing marring my happiness was the black spot, the sin, of having sent a traumatized woman bolting out of her life. For this, I still cannot forgive myself.

On one of the nights I spent running through the cool dark streets looking for Anais's Vanagon, Griselda shuffled to my door while I was gone to deliver a water-buckled copy of *Life and Fate* that she had discovered tossed by a Mountain View neighbor. She had seen my stash of books and knew how much I loved to read, she wrote in the lumpy copy, signing her full name. When she was returning through the gate, the mastiff, a strange puppyishness perhaps overwhelming him, rose up on his hind legs, all two hundred pounds of him, and put his two great paws on Griselda's shoulders, knocking the old woman down. In falling, she hit her head on one of the enormous geranium planters and something shifted and bubbled up inside her skull. The fall had also cut her scalp deeply, and a black pool of blood slowly grew on the stones behind her head. The dog would have barked his alarm, but could not. He skulked into the bamboo thickets, knowing he had done something terribly wrong. That night, I ran so far that I couldn't run anymore, and I walked home, cold and nearly blind with exhaustion. I picked up the book off my mat, entered the cottage, took a long hot shower, and slept until midmorning. When I came out to feed and water the mastiff, I saw through the bars of the gate the purple soles of Griselda's feet facing me. I rushed to her. Griselda was still alive, her eyes glassy. She was speaking. Oh, she murmured. It's you, the sun is bright. Wer rastet, der rostet. No, I am not fond of organ meat.

I ran inside, picked my way through the fetid piles of junk among which she must have burrowed for so many years, unable to feel, yet, the shock of the mess, and found her phone and called an ambulance. Then, back outside, I tried to press a towel on the wound of her scalp, but the blood had already clotted. She had rips on the shoulders of her nightgown, where the mastiff's claws had fallen, and a few bloody scratches on the skin beneath. The dog watched from the shadows, his chin on his paws.

While we waited, Griselda spoke, and amid her wild talk, her nonsense words, the long phrases in German, the directives to call her daughters, whose numbers were in the book by the phone, and to please please please, Liebchen, tidy up before the ambulance comes, she said two things that I later wrote down.

She said we have art so as not to die of the truth.

She said that in every human there is both an animal and a god wrestling unto death.

The first was Nietzsche. The second I have found nowhere. I think it was Griselda's own philosophy.

Griselda's daughters arrived while she was in the hospital. The doctors had induced a medical coma to help her brain heal, but the prognosis wasn't good. I had sent the mastiff to the pound; he had to be dragged out to the truck by two men, coughing his sad, soundless barks. He strained toward me as he passed, putting his cold nose on my leg, but I was too young to find in my heart any forgiveness for a murderer. I met the daughters when they at last came to their mother's home, after forty-eight hours at the hospital, when they were too exhausted to sit vigil at Griselda's side any longer.

They saw me waiting as they pulled into the drive, and got out of the car spiky with rage. Why weren't you here to check on her, they yelled, these skinny women dressed in expensive black. Why was that awful dog not under control? Why didn't anyone tell us she was so far gone? I kept my eyes down and said nothing. They went into Griselda's house. I couldn't move my body. They came out again, their faces crumbling at how their mother had been living. Sorry, they said. We're so sorry. It's not your fault. We're just so sad.

They stayed in a hotel for a month. One of the daughters would sit by Griselda, who was swollen and absent in her hospital bed, while the other put on work gloves and took armfuls of trash out to the hired skip. I stopped going to my job so that I could help with the clean-out, gathering up the newspapers and all sorts of things her neighbors had put out for trash and she had saved. We slowly uncovered the excellent furniture that had lain for so long beneath it all, which the daughters would be selling. We found treasures: Picasso prints, original Stickley chairs. One day, I unearthed a painting that had fallen behind a headboard in the guest room. Is this a Mondrian? I asked. The daughter gave a little crow. Oh! she said. It's here. We thought the robbers stole it. She hugged it to herself and took it back to her hotel room, and though I wanted to see it again, and would not, my hands still felt warm after having touched something so beautiful.

Only later did I realize that the daughter had mentioned the robbers, which meant that Griselda's story about them was likely true. I hadn't believed it. In truth, I hadn't believed any of her stories; they were all so composed, as if she had made them up long before. The daughters warmed to me, and began buying me sandwiches when it was time for lunch, and so one day I asked if the other stories that Griselda had told me were also true.

The daughter I was with that day, the one who wore expensive European glasses with tiny blue frames, looked at me with surprise. What stories? she said. I told her about Griselda's being the daughter of the industrialist in Germany, and how the toy store was opened just for her on Christmas Eve. Of her modeling career and of Andy Warhol. How she had been lost at sea for two weeks. How she'd been a philosopher at Princeton.

Then I saw, briefly, in the daughter's face a look of such yearning that I stopped talking. Yes, she said at last. All of this is true. Griselda doesn't lie, has never lied in her life.

Huh, I said.

No, you don't get it, the daughter said, blinking

quickly. It's just she never talked about any of it—any of it—with us. Even when we begged her to tell us. And yet she gave those stories to you, a total stranger.

Griselda never woke up. A truck came and took away the skip filled with junk. An auction house came and took away all the furniture. It turned out that underneath the furniture, the roots of the bamboo thickets had been pushing up through the terra-cotta floors. Griselda was cremated without a service. The daughters gave me one of the lesser Picasso prints and said I could stay in the cottage rent-free until the place was sold. I found a job as an administrative assistant at Stanford, basically a receptionist, with excellent health care.

Two months after Griselda died, a year into my quiet life alone in the cottage, I felt a disturbance in the air in front of my desk at work, and looked up, and standing there was a woman, and that woman was my mother. She wore a floral dress I had never seen before, and was cupping her hands to her mouth.

My mother said, I found you.

She had tracked me down through my Social Security number, which I'd given when applying for my job at Stanford. I left the office early. My mother looked deeply uncomfortable as we toured the cottage, and then she suggested that she rent a hotel room in the city. At first, there was a tension between us, a hesitancy, but she had always dreamed of San Francisco and had never been able to visit, and here she was, her face full of wonder, and the warmth between us returned, sweetened. We spent the weekend sightseeing. I have pictures of my mother on a trolley, eating a bread bowl full of chowder, in front of the Golden Gate Bridge in a sweatshirt she had to buy because she hadn't counted on it being so very cold in California. We split a bottle of wine the night before she flew back home, and she confessed that she thought I had been sucked into a prostitution ring or was on heroin or something, and she was going to have to rescue me, drag me home to that cold house with the wind coming through the drafty windows and too many children to a room.

No, I said. I'm finding my own way to survive.

For a long time she had nothing to say to that, then at last she gave a little shiver and said, It is so cold here. Aren't you so cold? I knew, obscurely, that she wasn't talking about the weather.

At the airport, she hugged me and cried, and just as she was about to go through security I watched as the new mother I had seen all weekend—bright, laughing, eager—changed physically, bending down to take off her shoes and coming up slightly slumped, shoulders rounded, as if already facing her chaotic home, her baffled husband and noisy children, and all the heaviness that awaited her there. I held my breath, but she didn't look back before she disappeared through the gate.

I HAD TO LEAVE the cottage not long after this. I moved away from the Bay Area a few years later. Life came for me, swallowed me up. I created my own family, and it has become my true north, which turns me in its direction no matter where I find myself, no matter all the changes that draw with astonishing swiftness over the face of the earth. Surely Anais's little girl is an adult now. I tell myself that with a mother as loving as Anais, surely she is fine. Still, the cottage, and Griselda's slowly sinking house, and even the vast and perfect oak tree, all of which took up an entire city block of the most expensive real estate in the country, must have been crushed and replaced by buildings meant for wealthier and more prosaic souls. I once lived in golden light in California, that light lived within me, and though it returns for spells here and there, that same golden light has never been with me as steadily as it was that year. In fact, there are often times when my life seems so small that the darkness in me has no outlet, and it keeps circling, faster and faster, tighter and tighter, until it seems that there is nothing but darkness, endlessly spinning. My emergence from these times is painful and very slow. I have to go far away to recover myself. My family has weathered these flights of mine before; they have learned to accept them, because in the past I have always returned, and when I do, I am a mother who sees her children fully.

In this pale apartment on another continent where I have come to be alone now, I have been waking, to my surprise, into brightness and peace, marveling that beauty could come so suddenly, after such deep and, I believed, permanent shadow. Grace is a gift undeserved, yet given anyway. In these hills I finally feel again that deep yearning, not for anything in particular but for the wild whole-being gladness that I knew for the first time in the cottage covered in moss and ferns and the shadow of the oak tree, where my freedom overwhelmed me. Sometimes when I am doing nothing but listening to the birds that nest in the crags of the nearby castle, I think about how there are, constellated through the countryside all around this place, churches full of Madonnas, paintings and frescoes and sculptures. There are a thousand Madonnas here, with a thousand different faces. Each Madonna wears the face of a particular mortal woman whom the artist loved. Each woman is one in whom the animal was briefly overcome by the god that lived within her.

Acknowledgments

Thank you to everyone at The Clegg Agency: the great Bill Clegg; the ferocious Marion Duvert; and Rebecca Pittel, Simon Toop, MC Connors, Sam Verney, and Andi Grene.

Thank you to everyone at Riverhead Books: Sarah McGrath and Corinne Leong in editorial; Claire McGinnis and Kitanna Hiromasa in publicity; Nora Alice Demick and Michelle Waters in marketing; Katie Hurley in production editorial; Caitlin Noonan and Maggie Kutz in managing editorial; Helen Yentus, Grace Han, and Lauren Peters-Collaer in cover design; Claire Vaccaro and Amanda Little in interior design; as well as Geoff Kloske and Jynne Dilling Martin.

Thank you to everyone at *The New Yorker*, in the pages of which most of these stories appeared. A special full-throated thanks to Cressida Leyshon and Deborah Treisman. Thank you to everyone at *The Atlantic*, especially Ann Hulbert. Thank you to Hannah Tinti and the team that put together *Small Odysseys*, as well as everyone at Selected Shorts. Thank you, *Best American Short Stories*, especially series editor Heidi Pitlor and guest editors Min Jin Lee and Andrew Sean Greer. Thank you, Word for Word in San Francisco, for performing "Annunciation" and showing me my own story as a prism.

Thank you, booksellers at The Lynx and at other independent bookstores, for the profound work of love that you do, and for being on the front lines of the fight for the freedom of expression.

Thank you to my family, nuclear and extended, including my boys' caregivers, camp counselors, grandparents, and teachers over the years that it took to write this collection. Without your time, patience, and brilliance, these stories wouldn't exist. Thank you, Beckett and Heath, for being so beautiful and strong and brave. Thank you, Clay, for being you.

Thank you, readers. Writers compose the score; readers make the music.

Author's Note on the Stories

The Wind

This story lived in my body before I even had language, passed down from my mother and my mother's mother. It was brought to the surface by a terrifying conversation with a stranger in the dark corner booth of a bar over twenty-five years ago, and finally flared into the heat and light of words through the steady application of time.

Between the Shadow and the Soul

Houses are bodies we build around ourselves and haunt like ghosts. The invisible third person in a marriage is the marriage itself.

To Sunland

The spirits can never stop moving in Florida because the limestone bedrock beneath is too fragile. Tacachale, which used to be called Sunland, is a mile from my house. On eerie nights—solstices, harvest moons—the house becomes a boulder in a stream, splitting a current of stirred-up former

Sunland spirits who are frantically looking for something. What, exactly, escapes them.

Brawler

I became a writer because I was a swimmer, spending hours every day dreaming while my body moved up and down the lanes, singing to myself, reciting poetry, doing complicated math, revising the life I'd already lived with far more wit and style. I feared and admired the divers, who, half birds, half fish, seemed at the same time suicidal and blazing with a courage too hot for soft, watery me to touch.

Birdie

There was a time long ago when I was ghosted by a group of people I believed to be close friends. It has been many years, but sometimes I'll walk around a corner and suddenly smash face-first into that old pain, which (unlike the rest of us) hasn't grown any older.

What's the Time, Mr. Wolf?

I used to believe that privilege was a poison. The more I live, though, the more I see that it's actually a fast-growing weed.

Under the Wave

I know a person who spent an entire week in Hawaii at a beach resort absolutely positive that a tsunami would roll in while she slept and swallow up the whole island, that she would awaken in a dark thrash, already drowning. I am not a fan of that person, who lives somewhere inside me.